To Debra.

Made For McKinley

Mavericks of Meeteetse, Book Two
Jonas & Ava

Renee Vincent

*Hope you enjoy this
all three books of
fun series!
all the best,
Renee Vincent*

Renee Vincent
P.O. Box 114
Alexandria, KY 41001

MADE FOR McKINLEY: (JONAS & AVA)
Copyright © 2015, Renee Vincent
Digital ISBN: 978-0-99673-630-5
Trade Paperback ISBN: 978-0-99673-634-3

Cover Art Design by Renee Vincent
Stock Art by BigStock.com
Editor, Linda Ingmanson

Digital Release: November, 2015
Trade Paperback Release: November, 2015

For my editor, Linda

I thank my luck stars that you took me on as one of your author clients. This series would not be what it is today without your careful, painstaking edits.
We make a great team!

MADE FOR McKINLEY
Mavericks of Meeteetse, Book 2 (Jonas & Ava)

Former trick rider Ava Wallace works the five-thousand-acre McKinley ranch and loves the man who owns it. Only trouble is, they've been living together for over seven years, and she can't help but think things have changed between them. Her rough-and-tough cowboy used to be relentless with his affection, unable to keep his hands off her. Now, he barely has the time.

Cowboy cattle rancher Jonas McKinley can't seem to catch a break. Between his hardworking live-in girlfriend feeling like they don't connect and the nuisance grizzly that keeps tormenting his livestock, he must overcome the troublesome challenges that threaten his lucrative family farm before he loses what he's worked so hard to keep. Faced with a difficult choice, Jonas has to decide what matters most: Ava or his ranch.

Chapter One

Ava Wallace watched the rugged cowboy dismount from his horse after a long day's work mending fence. A blue-and-white plaid shirt covered long, muscular arms. Short blond hair peeked out from beneath his white straw Stetson, while dark blond stubble shadowed his jaw. He had eyes as blue as denim and lashes as black as coal, a striking contrast to the lighter brows dusting his chiseled face. He came from Irish descent, at least on his father's side, but Ava swore he had a bit of Norse in him too.

Clad in tight jeans and weathered chaps, he led his faithful steed toward the east pasture gate. Dust wafted at his heels, and his handsome face glistened with perspiration under the Wyoming summer sun.

She had offered to go with him, but he was a stubborn man. From the many years working this five-thousand-acre ranch, she'd learned not to fight a losing battle. Men like him did not bend easily, nor did they back down at the first sign of trouble. Two hundred head of cattle threatening to roam free because of a broken fence was not necessarily an ordeal but something that came with the territory of being a modern-day cowboy.

Reckoning her chores could wait, Ava smiled as she continued to watch him from inside the barn. He might not have known it, but she enjoyed gazing at him. Everything he did was remarkable. Whether he tossed a bale of hay, roped a running steer, or simply leaned against a fence, he was worth watching.

She made herself more comfortable against the nearest barn post, while the spent cowboy made haste to cool himself at the water trough. She knew the ritual. First came the leather gloves.

He'd tug them off, then stuff them in his back pocket. After that, he'd remove his cowboy hat and swipe his brow with his sleeve. Replacing the Stetson atop his head, he'd lean against the blackboard fence and patiently wait as his horse, Winchester, drank.

As a man of habit, he did it all without fail.

Finally, Winchester lifted his head and shook his body. Dirt and grit clouded around both of them, but neither seemed to mind. In fact, the man praised his horse with a good pat on the neck. That gesture alone was one of the things she loved about him. He might have been a rough and tough cowboy on the outside, but inside he had an unashamed gentleness for the animals under his care.

Ava recalled the saying: *You can always tell how a man*

treats his woman by the way he treats his horse. She sighed and went back to mucking the horse stalls, reminiscing how she used to be on the receiving end of that cowboy's consideration—when he couldn't keep his hands off her. When he'd back her into a stall and kiss the daylights out of her every chance he got.

She missed those days.

When they'd first met seven years ago, nothing seemed to get in the way of their passionate, almost volatile relationship—not even his high-dollar working cattle ranch and all the responsibilities that came with it. Sure, the ranch had also grown into a booming horseback riding facility, thanks to Ava's previous trick riding skills on the rodeo circuit, but she never expected things to fizzle out between them.

Her cowboy Casanova went by the name of Jonas McKinley, known far and wide as the best cattle rancher in all of Wyoming. But to Ava, he was the reckless young stud who stole her heart.

Some say she stole his, as he was never the type to settle down. She and Jonas entertained a ten-year age difference, which helped her gain the dreaded *Colorado Cougar* title she'd heard going around the small town of Meeteetse from time to time. If anyone had done any thieving, it was the dashing, blue-eyed, hard-nosed heartthrob armed with the most perfect butt east of the Rockies.

Ava grinned at the thought of the first time she'd taken a long gander at Jonas McKinley's tight tush…

****

Seven years before present day

It was the week before the annual Cheyenne Frontier Days. At age thirty-three, it wasn't the first time Ava had entertained thousands of fans with her daredevil saddle stunts. But it was the first time her horse had come up lame.

As she stood in the stall, soaking Ranger's hoof in a bucket of warm water and Epsom salts, she heard the solid footsteps of a man. She looked up from under the brim of her hat and noticed a young, sexy cowboy strolling toward her. He looked like one of the many contestants who was there to win big money and fame, but she'd found out earlier that he was the contractor who provided the steers for all the events. It was quite an accomplishment for a man his age to obtain, and she could admit to being impressed.

But that was as far as her admiration carried her.

Though she'd seen him many times that week among

the chaos of preparations, she always avoided drawing his attention. Her Achilles' heel had been the obvious age difference between them. She had a teenage son who was closer to his age than her own, and she thought it downright immoral to take an interest in him.

Ducking her head to avoid any such eye contact, Ava returned to the task of tending her horse's hoof. Even if he did notice her, she never imagined a handsome, eligible twenty-something cowboy would give a woman with deepening crow's feet the time of day. She thought he'd walk right by her.

A whistle broke the silence and then his voice. "Now, that's a nasty abscess."

Ava nearly jumped out of her jeans, dropping Ranger's hoof in the bucket. Water splashed her face, but her horse barely flinched and continued to munch on the hay hanging from a canvas bag in the corner. She clutched her chest and blew out a heavy breath. "Jesus, you startled me!"

"My bad." He sported a beautiful smile as he held out his hand. "And the name's Jonas, not Jesus."

Ava smiled back as she wiped the water droplets from her face, reluctant to make physical contact with him. Eventually, she shook his hand because she liked his sense of humor. "Jonas McKinley, right?"

"That's right."

Ava felt her hand tremble and jerked it away before he could notice.

Calm down, Ava. It's not like he's George Strait or something.

"Sorry if I scared you," he said, glancing at the way she fiddled with her shirt. "I didn't think you trick riders balked at anything."

Ava cleared her throat, surprised that he knew her profession. What surprised her more was how his simple touch did crazy things to her. Things she hadn't felt in a long time. Things that felt completely inappropriate right now.

Remember, Ava. He's just a man. Nothing special.

She forced her brain to articulate a blasé version of the guy. Dwelling on everything else that came to mind darn near killed her. She smiled. "You must have us confused with the bull riders. They're the fearless ones."

"I don't know. I think slinging your body upside down on a sprinting horse requires its own set of balls." He grinned and winked. "Pardon my French."

Ava laughed at his apology, though she'd heard worse things come from the mouths of bronc riders. "Well, for the record, I've never had a set of balls. So, I guess my excuse for riding beneath the belly of a horse is just plain idiocy."

He crossed his arms, then his ankles, and leaned

against the stall gate. "Skillful bravery maybe. But not idiocy."

"Call it what you want, Mr. McKinley, but it doesn't look like I'll be displaying either this time around." She sighed and glanced at her horse standing in a bucket. "I think the farrier quicked him."

"That's a damn shame."

She patted her horse and nodded. "I know. The farrier's a good friend of my late father, so this is not going to be an easy conversation to have with him."

"Late father, huh? I lost mine too. I'm sorry to hear about that."

"No, it's okay. It was a long time ago. Really."

"Well, it's still a damn shame. A shame I won't get to see you in spandex. Especially that black-and-silver one I saw you practicing in the other day. I think it's my favorite."

Ava felt her face flush. She could hardly look at him.

Did he really like the look of her body poured into that slick black-and-silver outfit or just all females in general who trick rode? At his age, she assumed the latter and reminded herself not to get her hopes up. The chances of him finding her even remotely sexy were slim to none. She chewed on her lip.

"My apologies if I came off too forward, ma'am."

Ava cringed at the sound of the sweet Southern drawl punctuating his confession. It wasn't the way he said it, but the title with which he chose to address her.

Ma'am.

Ugh! Ma'am is for proper older ladies. She was neither proper, nor old—at least she didn't feel old. Mature, maybe, but not old.

"What's with the face?" He leaned over the stall gate, and the cords in his neck tightened. Her gaze drew past the collar of his plaid Western shirt onto what she imagined to be warm, smooth skin. "Did I say something wrong?"

Her eyes met his, and she turned to mush. Looking into his crystalline eyes made her heart yearn for the tenderness of a man's sympathetic gaze. It had been a long time since she'd looked into the eyes of a handsome man. Far too long…

Ava quickly glanced away and shook off her ridiculous emotions.

Buck up, Ava. Don't let this green cowboy fluster you.

She straightened her back and stood her ground. No tantalizing tadpole was going to refer to her as old. "I'd rather you not call me ma'am."

He drew back and furrowed his brow. A cocky little smirk inched up the corner of his mouth as if he enjoyed her sudden feistiness. "My mama always taught me to be polite when talking to a woman, no matter how bad I wanna kiss her. So until you tell me what your name is, I'll be forced to continually unsettle you." He leaned closer. "And just so we're clear, I'd rather say things to arouse you."

Ava wasn't prepared for that comeback and could barely get past *"how bad I wanna kiss her."* Was he serious?

She shoved her hands in the pockets of her jeans so he wouldn't see her shaking.

"Ma'am?" he prompted. "Your name?"

Ava blinked repeatedly and forced herself back to reality. She looked at Jonas slouching with his elbows resting on the gate, his hands folded. The unabashed confidence he portrayed in his casual posture was more than she could handle. Younger or not, he was clearly more experienced in flirtatious dialogue.

"I'm sorry. My name is Ava. Ava Wallace."

He stood up straight and tipped his hat, his smile as broad as an arena barn. "Pleasure to meet you, Ava. Now, since I already struck a chord with you, I reckon I'll strike another."

"Excuse me?"

"Your horse. You seem pretty partial toward him, and I get that. If you're in need of a backup for the show this week, you're welcome to use mine. In his prime, he was a trick mount, but I bought and trained him to be a cutting horse. It's been about five years since he's galloped in a pen, but he's as sound as they come. He'll run like mad till you tell him to stop. Bomb goes off? Won't flinch a muscle. Dead broke."

He stroked the stubble on his jaw, and her attention zeroed in on his large hand. Ava imagined he probably knew a thing or two about how to properly use those strong, beautiful hands on a woman and how she'd give anything to be *that* woman.

"Obviously, you'll want to test him and see how he does running the pattern, but I'm thinking he'll have you saying 'hell yeah.'"

Ava dismissed the thoughts of his roaming hands and pretended to be indifferent. "That's a mighty nice offer, Mr. McKinley."

"Call me Jonas," he corrected. "Like you, I don't care to be called by stiff-collar titles."

"Okay."

"If you decide to take me up on my offer," he explained, pointing toward the corrals lining the rodeo grounds, "I'll be right over there."

Ava glanced in the direction he pointed. "Got it."

Jonas tipped his hat once more and strolled away, leaving her to ponder. And stare…

She took in his view from behind and nearly drooled. *It should be illegal for a man to have a butt like that.*

"Wooo, doggy, I agree. That fine butt *should* be illegal."

Ava whirled at the sound of a voice behind her. Her friend and fellow barrel racer, Crystal—or as she insisted, Crys, because the other was just too feminine—stood on the other side of the stall, her chin resting on the tops of her hands. Unlike Ava, Crys made no attempt to hide her gawking.

Ava covered her mouth in horror. "Did I seriously say those words out loud?"

"Yes, ma'am, you did." Crystal quickly looked in her direction and amended her statement. "I mean, Ava."

Ava rolled her eyes. "How long have you been eavesdropping?"

"Long enough to know his mama taught him right and he's dying to kiss you." Crystal giggled. "Or arouse you."

Ava shook her head and bent to check on Ranger's hoof. "Obviously, your mama never taught *you* right."

"Ah, now don't get your knickers in a bunch. I'm not gonna tell anyone that you got the hots for Mr. Sweet Tush over there. And you do, so don't deny it."

When it came to Crys, nothing slid past her. She came from a long line of bull riders, which meant she took no bull from anybody. A lie to her was as easily detected as a skunk in roses. Ava also knew the woman had loyalty, given they'd traveled the rodeo circuits together for over eleven years.

She recalled on one occasion how Crys had punched some cocky bull rider square in the nose for a degrading comment he made toward a young newbie barrel racer. He thought he was a big shot in front of his friends. Crys thought he needed to be put in his place.

Ava almost laughed, remembering how he'd mounted a longhorn steer the next day wearing a face-guard helmet. While it wasn't uncommon for a bull rider to protect his face from fracture in a competition, this guy never did— until that day. Irony was often a gifted comedian.

"So, what are you gonna do about McKinley's offer?" Crys asked as she spread shavings in her stall.

Ava lifted Ranger's leg and pulled the bucket away, ready to salve and Vetrap the hoof. "I don't know. It sounds pretty dangerous to me."

"Are you talking about the man's horse or his kiss?"

Ava contemplated the question. "Both, I reckon."

Crys threw down the last of the shavings with a very devious grin. "I can't speak for borrowing another man's horse, but I don't think a kiss ever killed anyone."

Chapter Two

Ava settled back in the saddle after finishing an easy horn twirl on Jonas McKinley's horse. She slipped her feet back into the stirrups just in time to pull the reins. Winchester slowed his gallop and hopped atop the soft dirt until he came to a stop.

"Nice ridin', Trick," Jonas said.

Ava dismounted and smiled at Jonas, who was leaning against the stadium entrance gate. She couldn't help it, especially since he'd already come up with a nickname for her in less than a few hours. Trick was definitely a whole lot better than ma'am.

She clutched the reins beneath Winchester's chin and led him forward. "Thanks for letting me ride him. He's definitely as good as you say." She patted the quarter horse's neck, the familiar smell of warm, sweaty equine hide filling her senses.

Jonas pushed off the post and took two steps, stopping right in front of her. His height was immense. At five foot seven, she barely stood eye to eye with his shoulders.

"Does that mean you're comfortable enough to use him?"

"With all due respect, Mr. McKinley—"

"I insist you call you me Jonas."

Ava felt her heart skip. Between his towering presence and his husky voice, akin to something he'd use in the bedroom, she could barely think. She swallowed hard. The dusty dirt she'd inhaled on the practice runs did nothing to aid the dryness in her throat. She'd give anything for a cold beer right now.

"Right. Jonas," she amended. "I appreciate the offer and the fact that you're willing to let me test him. But I can't afford to use just any horse and risk breaking my neck. There's a relationship between rider and horse, which I'm sure you can relate to given he's a cutting horse. Dead broke as he may be, I can't assume he'll run the pattern without fail while I'm stretched out in a hippodrome stand. I need a horse who's trained for such things."

"So, train him."

"In a week's time?" She didn't mean to scoff, but it just came out. "Look, I realize he was once a trick mount, but that doesn't mean it'll all come back to him. He's a horse, not an elephant."

Jonas shot a glance toward Winchester and stroked his muzzle. "He can hear you, you know."

Ava laughed. "Again, I mean no disrespect to you or your horse. He's a remarkable animal. But I can't afford an injury at this stage in my life. If I can't ride, I don't get paid. And I have college to pay for."

Jonas's eyes widened. "College, huh? Whatcha studying?"

She prepared herself for what she knew would come to pass anyway. Once he found out she was old enough to have a kid in college, he'd hightail it out of sight. "I'm not studying anything. My son, Sawyer, is. Well, will be. In a couple of years. He's a freshman at Hadberry High."

For the first time since they'd met, she had the balls to look Jonas in the eye. Her son was the most important person in her life, and she'd be damned if she'd let some smooth-talking, eye-catching cowboy weasel his way in and try to change that. She half expected to see Jonas stutter and stammer like a man standing on hot coals.

But he didn't.

He just smiled, his emotions unreadable. Was that adoration twinkling in his eyes or a look of smugness? And what was there to be smug about? Was he thinking that charming his way into a mother's heart was a bigger trophy than scoring with some shameless buckle bunny? Whatever he thought, it was never going to happen.

"Really? You have a teenage son?"

She raised my chin proudly. "I do."

"I would've never guessed. You've aged gracefully. Like sweet wine."

Ava assumed that was a compliment she should be happy about, but given the subject had to do with her growing old, it didn't feel like one—no matter how sexy he said it.

His eyes narrowed and he cleared his throat. "So, where's *Mister* Wallace?"

"Heck if I know." She shrugged. "I haven't seen or heard from him since I told him I was pregnant."

Jonas's face softened with sincerity. "He didn't want to be in his son's life?"

"We were sixteen. And his highfalutin parents had a promising future planned for him. They said a baby would ruin that. So, he signed over his rights and that was it."

"Hmm..." he murmured, shoving a thumb in his pocket. "Any man who doesn't take responsibility for his own actions is a coward. I hate to say this, Trick, but your son's better off without him. He deserves a real role model, like his hard-working mama, for instance."

Now, that was a compliment. And she couldn't argue with Jonas about the *sperm donor* being a coward. He'd been that and more, especially since Sawyer was the son who would make any father proud.

Despite the absence of a father in Sawyer's life, he'd grown to be a strong, intelligent, and ethical young man—a real gentleman, with aspirations of pursing a bachelor's degree in Business and Equine Management at the University of Kentucky after high school graduation. Often times, he'd travel with her during the summer months, as long as his extracurricular schedule allowed for it. But this was one of those times when it didn't. Currently, he stayed with her mother in Colorado, and although she spoke to him on a regular basis, she missed him greatly. Everything she did was for Sawyer. She wanted the best for him, which brought her back to the reason she couldn't borrow Jonas's horse.

"I hope you understand why I must decline your generous offer, and I hope there are no hard feelings. It's nothing personal, I assure you. It's just that trick riding is dangerous enough on a horse I'm familiar with."

Jonas stepped closer, keeping his left hand on Winchester's muzzle. He stroked it absently, never taking his eyes from hers. "I completely understand. The last thing I'd want is for you to get hurt."

Ava saw his gaze drop to her lips. The glance was understated enough that most women wouldn't have noticed it. But she did. Despite her efforts, she zeroed in on lots of things Jonas did. Like the way he always petted an animal the minute he was within reach. Or the way a dimple appeared from the slightest grin. Nothing was too subtle for her.

"So, if you won't take my horse, can I offer you something else?" His voice took on a sensual yet raspy nature. "Something hot...a little sticky sweet, maybe."

"I beg your pardon?"

"Coffee and apple pie." His dimples popped out this time. "Care to join me?"

Jonas was definitely a showstopper with that beautiful smile. She'd say yes to just about anything that man asked her should he flash those pearly whites. But why would he want to hang out with her? She'd been out of the dating scene for more time than she cared to admit, and she knew the stages of common courtship hadn't changed all that much.

Talking led to getting to know each other.

Getting to know each other led to comfortableness.

Comfortableness dangerously led to no inhibitions, and eventually boredom.

Although she swore her virginity had grown back because of how long it had been since she'd knocked boots with a man, she knew exactly where things ended up when inhibitions were gone. And she was just too old to put herself in a position where she might get hurt.

As great as a cup of coffee sounded, Ava held firm like the fastened hand of a bull rider. "I feel awful for turning you down again, but—"

"So don't," he quickly argued. "Say yes. That way you won't feel awful and I won't feel shot down. It's a win-win for both of us."

She twirled a loose strand of hair and closed her eyes, trying to figure out if having a cup of coffee with this guy would complicate things. Behind tight lids, she tried to block everything out and make a sound decision based on the moral high rode, but instead she imagined Jonas pulling her into a kiss hot enough to melt Arizona asphalt.

At the sound of her own whimper, Ava's eyes flew open. Jonas's expression projected confusion and wonder, with a slight hint of amusement.

"You all right?"

She quickly covered her mouth, mortified that her daydream had caused her to react in ways that mimicked an actual kiss. She cleared her throat and rolled her shoulder, pretending to wince. "Yeah, this dang shoulder. I guess I shouldn't be surprised with as many years as I've put into this trick riding gig."

"You might have a torn rotator."

He reached for her shoulder, but she shrugged him off. "It's fine, really."

"You sure? By the sound of that noise you made, I think it hurts a lot more than you let on."

"Seriously, it's nothing." Ready to use anything to redirect his attention from her fake shoulder strain to something else, that cup of joe suddenly didn't seem so bad after all. "So, how about that coffee, Jonas? I think I could really use some now."

"Yeah?" He looked totally confused.

"Yeah. I mean, what could it hurt? It's just coffee and dessert. Right?"

"Are you asking my opinion? Or still trying to convince yourself?" He looked at her more shrewdly this time, his blue eyes piercing.

She bit her lip. "Maybe both?"

Ava supposed he was a lot smarter than she gave him credit for. He seemed to read her like a book, though she couldn't begin to speculate one thing about him. So far, everything she assumed about this guy was dead wrong. And here she thought herself a great judge of character. Perhaps she was out of practice. Or better yet, Mr. Tall Drink of Water was just the kind of man she needed to keep her on her toes.

He took the reins from her hand and turned his horse

in a one-eighty. "How about you walk with me to the barn so I can untack Winchester, and then we can talk more about our coffee date. In the meantime, you think about why we shouldn't be seen together. If you can come up with one viable excuse…" He paused and turned to look slightly over his shoulder. He readjusted the cowboy hat on his head, his gaze hitting her like blue fire. "And I *do* mean viable. As in…it would be impossible for me to argue with you. If you can do that, then I'll walk away."

Jonas didn't wait for her to answer, or give her a chance to debate it. He strolled out of the arena and led Winchester down the exit chute.

Was this guy for real?

And since when did coffee and apple pie mean a date?

Ava looked around, wondering if anyone had paid attention to their little discussion. She saw a few workers in the stands, wiping down the bleachers. A handful of men assembled a new red gate for the bronc and bull chutes. A crew of excavators delivered a dump truck load of fill dirt, and a guy on a tractor waited to spread it.

The closest person within earshot was a cute little blonde barrel racer exercising her horse with a lunge line. If *anyone* had paid attention to Jonas, it would've been her— the eligible female. But no one seemed particularly interested in anything that had transpired between her and the hunky cowboy. And he paid no mind to whether she was following him or not.

She scoffed and crossed her arms. Jonas had her feeling like she was supposed to say *how high* whenever he said *jump*. Since when did she ever listen to a man? She never listened to Sawyer's father's selfish demands. Why start now?

Ava breathed in a harsh, ragged breath and swiped the fuzzy hairs away from her forehead. Though Jonas's dominance didn't sit well with her, she still felt a restlessness in her legs that wanted to carry her in his direction.

Finally, she gave in, realizing she looked more ridiculous standing in the arena alone than catching up with him.

Despite her urge to run, she forced herself to walk.

Casually.

One deliberate step after another.

How could one man have such a profound effect on her? So much that she was practically turning into one of those googly-eyed female rodeo fans clinging to the fence for a chance to meet a cowboy. She reminded herself that she was the woman on the other side of the fence, riding horses in a way most wouldn't dare. She needed to take charge of herself and not allow Jonas to dictate her actions, no matter how much he flustered her.

With determination in her stride, Ava turned the corner and exited the arena. She followed the whiteboard fence toward the barn where Jonas stalled Winchester. On her way there, she practiced her words in her head. She was determined not to be tongue-tied in front of him.

By the time she entered the barn, Jonas had already led Winchester into his stall and was about to step inside. She rushed forward and grabbed him by the arm. His bicep flexed beneath her grip, hard and bulging. He flicked his gaze in the direction of her grasp as if surprised by her audacity. A slow, easy grin spread across his lips. Inside, her stomach knotted.

She released his arm immediately and slipped between him and the stall door, taking back control of the situation she'd gotten herself into. "Where I come from, the rider is expected to untack the horse."

Without looking back, Ava stroked Winchester's hindquarter upon her approach and made quick work of the girth. She felt Jonas watching her, the heat of his stare bearing down on her back.

Thank goodness this is my saddle. I could do this in my sleep.

Next, she figured this was the perfect opportunity to lay some groundwork.

"I know you may think you can throw your weight

around in my presence, but that's not how this is going down. I'm not some inexperienced female you can have your way with. I've got a few years on you. That said, I'm the one who's leery about getting involved with a man who's still wet behind his ears. If you want my company so badly, then *you* should be the person to convince me. Not the other way around."

After unhooking the chest, girth, and buck strap, Ava grabbed the pad and saddle together and swung it off Winchester's back. Facing Jonas, she stiffened her spine. "So, convince me, if you think you can."

It felt good to lasso the steer called Submissive and hog-tie it right before his eyes. He stood still, arms crossed, his smile as big as ever. Her confidence wavered slightly as he looked like a bull ready to mow her down.

"You want me to convince you." He stated it as a reiterative, rather than asking if that was the objective. His smile disappeared, though his gaze remained. He looked more determined now.

Suddenly, she didn't think she could win this battle of wills with Jonas McKinley, but she gave it all she had.

"Yes. Try and convince me."

She stepped forward to move past him, but he yanked the saddle from her hands and threw it on the rack outside the stall. Dangling stirrups thudded against the wood as he dusted off his hands.

"Challenge accepted."

He lunged forward, his body forcing her back into the privacy of Winchester's stall until she hit the solid oak wall behind her. He braced his hands on either side of her head. His eyes darkened. He stared at her gaping mouth as if trying to assure himself that kissing the feistiness out of her might be a good idea. He didn't struggle with the notion very long.

He dipped his head and sealed his mouth over hers. His tongue slipped in, caressing her, tasting her. She melted at the pleasure of this man's kiss, as he certainly knew his way around one.

He then pulled slowly out of the kiss and leaned his forehead against hers. A long, shaky exhale and a boyish grin split his lips. "How's that? Was that convincing enough for you?"

Chapter Three

Trapped behind Jonas's hard, virile body, Ava couldn't escape the smell of his cologne mixed with a slight hint of perspiration. She didn't know anything about pheromones, but she was certain his scent alone was an aphrodisiac.

She swallowed and tried to play it cool, despite her strong desire to kiss him again. "Am I supposed to want coffee at this moment?"

His quiet laughter rumbled through his chest. "The only thing I *want* right now is to kiss you again. If you'll let me."

His mouth moved over hers and he kissed her again. This time, it was even slower and more sensual. He explored every inch of her mouth as if it was the last time he'd ever kiss her.

Would this be the last time?

Would she have the strength to turn him away now that a significant line had been crossed? The very thought was impossible to determine with his body pressing against hers.

"What's wrong?" he asked heatedly, as if he heard her questioning where they go from here in his own head.

Ava gently pushed at his chest with both hands. "I can't do this."

"Can't do what?"

She tried to gesture between the limited space he left. "This. You and me. It's wrong. It's *so* wrong. It can't happen."

"Why? What's so wrong about it? You got a boyfriend?"

"No."

A smile inched on his face and one dimple popped out with his next question. "You're a lesbian?"

"No!"

"Then what is it?"

She huffed aloud, frustrated that he played dumb. He knew darn well what the issue was. "I'm too old for you, Jonas." He opened his mouth to speak, but she covered it. "Yes, I am. And you know it."

"Then why'd you let me kiss you?"

His warm breath tickled her palm, and she felt the sensation all the way down to her toes. She jerked her hand from his mouth, but he snatched her wrist.

"You should've slapped me, Trick, but instead, you

kissed me back. Admit it, you wanted me to."

Ava looked away. She felt weak and full of shame for what she wanted. He was just too young for her to crave those things from him. She couldn't help but feel she'd only be taking advantage. She had to resist Jonas McKinley. It was best for both of them.

Just walk out.

"Look at me, Ava."

He spoke in a whisper, a satiny susurrus laced with grit. That intoxicating sound alone willed her to move. Like ribbons of grass bending in the wind, she had no choice but to shift her gaze in his direction. His warm, kind eyes hit her like the double-barrel hind kick of a horse. His face had softened to match the rich, dulcet tone of his voice. She fell limp under his spell as he brushed the wispy hair from her face.

"You and I are so much alike, it's scary. We both have rules we hate to break. And until you came along, I never broke them."

He looked at his horse and stepped back. The buckle of Winchester's throatlatch became his focus instead of her face. She was thankful for the reprieve and equally curious about Jonas's rules.

"What rules did you break with me?"

In one fluid motion, he reached beneath the horse's

jaw and up to the opposite ear, sliding off the headstall. Winchester opened his mouth as the bit fell out. Jonas gave the horse a good pat on the neck and turned to face her. His eyes enchanted her again.

"Number one, I never let anyone ride my horse. And that means no one."

Ava pursed her lips, hiding a grin. She wasn't sure what special factor she had to make him forgo that rule, but she liked it.

"Number two?" she prompted.

"I never get involved with anyone from the rodeo circuit. That includes those who ride and those who watch."

"So why me?" She couldn't believe she actually voiced her thoughts. Engaging this man in conversation was not the way to brush him off.

And did she really want to know? What if it was because of a dare? Or a bet? Men did that crap all the time. Would she be able to handle his reason if it were on the sharp side of a wager?

Probably not.

Jonas took hold of her hand and captured her with his gaze. She could see the sincerity expressed in the magnificent swirl of blue in his eyes.

"Why did I break rules for you, Trick? Because I can't

stop myself. I'd break every rule there was just to be close to you."

Chapter Four

Present day

"Hey, Trick. You about ready to go inside? I'm beat."

Jonas's voice pulled Ava from her reverie, and she looked up, her manure rake still in her hand. He stood at the stall door, regarding her progress or lack thereof.

"Whatcha been doing?"

Daydreaming of you, she thought.

"I figured you'd have had this finished by now."

"Sorry, I guess I'm just tired." Which wasn't a lie. While Jonas had been fixing fence, Ava had unloaded a flatbed trailer full of square bales and stacked them in the barn. Normally, she'd have had help with this chore, but it was Sunday. According to Jonas, no one worked on Sunday. Evidently, that rule only applied to the hired hands.

"I see Mr. Corinth delivered the hay a day early," he said. "You should've called me. I would have helped you."

Ava scraped up the last pile of wet shavings and horse

manure, and scooped it into the wheelbarrow. She appreciated the fact that he worried about her. At least she cultivated some sort of awareness, even if it was only in retrospect.

"I was perfectly capable."

Laying the rake on top, she attempted to push the wheelbarrow out of the stall, but Jonas nudged her aside.

"I got this."

She stepped back, letting him maneuver the heavy pile of waste down the barn aisle. Her aching back thanked him.

Ava followed him outside, stretching as she walked. She glanced at the tight butt emphasized in his chaps, and it still looked as perfect as the day they had met. In the middle of her last stretch, she checked out her own backside, wondering if Jonas could say the same. Wondering if he even still looked at it.

"So, what happened to Mr. Corinth's arm?" he asked.

Ava cleared her throat and scratched her head, trying to redirect her thoughts from her butt to Mr. Corinth's fractured limb. "How did *you* know about it?"

"His wife called me while I was fixing fence. She said he broke his elbow but didn't give up all the details. She was more concerned with bribing me."

"Bribing you? For what?" A funny thought ran through Ava's mind. "*With* what?" she amended.

Jonas glanced over his shoulder and flashed a grin. "Couple of her apple pies in exchange for helping Mr. Corinth with his next cutting. It seems she's rallying all the neighbors. But I have to keep my mouth shut about it. If Mr. Corinth finds out, he'll throw a fit."

Everyone in Meeteetse, Wyoming knew Mrs. Corinth and her mouthwatering apple pies. No one stood a chance of saying no when her prize-winning pastries were the payoff. "I'd say that's a mighty sweet deal for your secrecy."

"An easy one too. I don't talk to that man any more than I have to."

"Is that why it took you all day to fix fence? Sounds to me like you *knew* he was coming to drop off that hay."

Jonas laughed at her joke. Anyone within a hundred-mile radius of Meeteetse knew Mr. Corinth was a talker. If he could hook just an inkling of your attention, you'd better saddle up for the long haul. He'd talk your ear off till dawn if you let him.

Ava wondered how Mrs. Corinth survived all those years of him bumping his gums. She imagined marital bliss for the missus was when the man slept.

"Nah, I wouldn't do that to you," Jonas said, "To Cole, I would. But not you."

Cole Forester and Jonas went way back, and it felt good to know she ranked high enough to dodge the evil tricks the two friends constantly played on each other.

"Is that why you fell behind today?" Jonas asked. "Mr. Corinth?"

Blaming Mr. Corinth sounded like a great excuse. Better than admitting she was lost in a daydream about when they first met. But she was a horrible liar. "Not really."

He handed her the rake, and she watched him tip the wheelbarrow beneath the covered roof of the manure pit. He looked at her curiously as a hint of a grin tugged at the corner of his lip. One of his dimples threatened to surface.

"So what was it, then?"

Ava hung the rake on the wall and shoved her hands in the back pockets of her jeans. How was she supposed to explain herself? How was she supposed to tell Jonas McKinley, the cowboy who swore he'd never settle down, that she missed the way things used to be? That they'd gotten too comfortable with their relationship and needed to make improvements. That they should spice things up a bit.

How could she say all that when she was lucky enough to snag him anyway?

She should've possessed enough pride to know he was just as lucky to have *her*. But the truth was that this was Jonas's first serious relationship. By confessing her woes, she feared she was about to shoot herself in the foot and lose the one thing she needed most.

Ava cut the dirt with the tip of her boot, staring at the line she drew in the loose soil. She felt ridiculous feeling this way. She felt ungrateful wishing for more from Jonas when every other woman would've given her left arm to have what she had. By the same token, she felt like she deserved more. She wasn't just a warm body for the bedroom and a strong back for the barn.

"Ava?" His hand came up to her cheek. He stroked his thumb across her skin and contemplated her silence. Without having to ask, he seemed to realize something was amiss. "You're upset with me."

She fidgeted. "I'm not upset—"

"Yes, you are. I can see it." He tapped his fingertip at her temple. "This little vein right here gives it away."

"Is that right?" She tried to fake her composure, but it was impossible with him so close. She could practically feel the heat from his body reaching out to her, coaxing her into his arms. After seven years with this man, he still got to her. His sheer presence had all her nerve endings on high alert, dying to feel the connection of his touch. She wondered if her proximity ever affected him. Judging by the mild complacency on his handsome face, she doubted it.

"Come on, Trick. What's bothering you?"

She took a deep breath. "Do you ever think... I mean, *I've* been thinking... Well, I guess I mean more like I've been wondering..."

His laughter cut her off. "Spit it out already."

"I'm trying. It's just hard to explain without sounding ridiculous." She sidestepped him to put some distance between them. "Jonas... Do you ever feel like we're too comfortable with each other?"

His hands went to his hips, and his brow furrowed as he processed it. "Comfortable with each other?"

She watched him adjust his hat on his head, as if that gave the idea more wiggle room in his brain.

"Yes, comfortable," she reiterated.

"Isn't that a good thing? I thought women wanted their men to be comfortable with them. Should I not be comfortable around you?"

"What I mean is *too* comfortable."

He looked even more perplexed. "*Too* comfortable. Okay..." His gaze lifted toward the sky as if he were trying to find the correct answer in the heavens. "I have no clue what you're trying to say here, Trick. Comfortable—too comfortable. What's the problem with that? You and I, we're comfortable with each other. So what?"

"So, I feel like we're not as close as we used to be."

It sounded perfectly logical to her.

"You want us to be closer," he guessed reservedly, still unsure. "Yet, we're *too* comfortable together. Does that even make sense?"

His cell phone rang, interrupting their discussion. She sighed as he lifted his index finger for her to pause while he pulled it from his pocket and checked the caller. He grumbled and closed his eyes.

"Great. It's Mr. Corinth."

The irritating ringtone blared a couple more times in his hand as he looked at Ava for permission. She wondered if he really felt the need to answer the call or if he was using it as an excuse to dodge their conversation. Either way, it didn't much matter. She and Jonas were on two different planets when it came to issues of the heart.

"Fine. Just answer it."

Before he hit the button, he snagged her arm, pulling her attention to his handsome face. "We'll finish this inside. Okay?"

Ava nodded, thankful that he seemed interested enough in her miseries to continue the conversation later. "Okay. I'll go make dinner."

He swiped a peck from her lips and assured her he wouldn't be long. He turned to connect the call and greeted their neighbor with his drawn-out version of "hello," which always came out sounding like "yellow." As she walked toward the house, she could hear his conversation with Mr. Corinth.

"Yeah, I saw you delivered the hay. Mmmhmm...yeah. Yeah. I reckon. Mmmhmm. Huh. You broke your arm, did ya?"

Ava had to laugh, because she knew the last thing Jonas wanted was to get knee-deep in a conversation with Mr. Corinth about how it happened. Hearing Jonas fall silent, she knew Mr. Corinth had already begun to describe the incident with explicit detail. With Mr. Corinth, there was no such thing as a shortened version.

She glanced over her shoulder just in time to see Jonas kick up dust with his boot and frisbee his hat across the yard in frustration, all the while feigning interest in the long-drawn-out tale.

That was her gentleman cowboy, right there. All spit and fire on the inside, charming and courteous on the outside.

Chapter Five

By the time Jonas entered the house, Ava had a platter of grilled pork chops, red potatoes, and carrots on the kitchen table. The look on his face foretold a very lengthy, brutal phone call from Mr. Corinth.

"Remind me next time to let voice mail answer all calls from that man."

She shot him a look of pity as he hung his hat on the wall rack and toed off his cowboy boots. "That bad, huh?"

"Let's just say I thought I'd walk in here and you'd have breakfast on the table." He walked past her and entered the kitchen, flipping on the faucet to wash his hands. "I feel so sorry for his wife. How that woman puts up with his long-winded chatter is beyond me. I wouldn't be surprised if she were the one who pushed him down the stairs."

"He broke his arm falling down the stairs?"

"That's what he claims. Said he was carrying a box of empty canning jars when he lost his footing on the cellar steps."

"Oh my gosh." Ava suddenly felt a pang of sympathy for the old man. At his age, it was a wonder he didn't break more than just his right arm. "He could've cracked his head wide open on those concrete steps."

"Not to mention Mrs. Corinth's jars," he joked, drying his hands on a dish towel. "I doubt he'd be alive to tell the tale if he had."

Ava giggled at his jest, though she knew Mrs. Corinth adored her husband. "Come on and eat. It's getting cold. And turn your cell on vibrate in case he tries to call again."

"Already did."

Jonas didn't hesitate to sit down. He drew in a long whiff and rubbed his empty belly as he scooted in his chair. "I love you, Ava."

She sat across from him, smiling at how easily pleased he was by the sight of a home-cooked meal. She guessed the old saying was true after all. Of course, she'd known the way to a man's heart was through his stomach long before she could cook. She'd seen her mother use her culinary skills for her own benefit many times, though Ava could honestly say it wasn't to gain her father's affection. Her mother's kickback was often times more materialistic. If she wanted something that Father would likely say no to, all she had to do was cook him a pot roast with all the trimmings, and her wish was as good as granted.

What Ava also learned from her father was her independence. He always said she should never rely on a man to take care of her. While it was certainly great advice growing up, especially with a child on the way at sixteen, she realized later that it was more likely due to the fact that he didn't think *any man* was worthy of taking care of his daughter.

Secretly, she wondered what her father, God rest his soul, would think of Jonas. Would he approve of her choice in the young cattle rancher? While Jonas had a way of making an honest living and supporting her ventures along the way, she still had needs that weren't exactly being met.

Ava had to smile as she realized her troubles weren't something she could discuss with her father even if he were alive to hear them. This was something she had to figure out on her own. Knowing Jonas as well as she did, it wasn't going to be easy.

Once their napkins hit their laps, Ava and Jonas bowed their heads and said grace. As always, she thanked God for her many blessings but sent a silent prayer to Him for the strength to get through this discussion without losing the man she loved.

After their amens, she watched Jonas pick up his utensils and cut his meat. A smile of intense satisfaction hit his lips as he savored his first bite.

"Ava? If I didn't know better, I'd say your cooking outweighs your trick ridin'."

"Lucky for you, I hung that hat up years ago."

"Wasn't *that* long ago," he said before shoveling in another bite of meat and potatoes.

Ava laughed. "Seven years is a long time, Jonas."

She cringed after saying that, because that was exactly how long she and Jonas had been together. Was seven years really a lengthy stretch of time? If they were too comfortable with each other after seven years, what would they be in another seven?

"Do you ever miss it?" he asked.

She took longer cutting her meat as she pondered his question. When she thought about trick riding, it seemed that it always came back to when she and Jonas met. She could hardly think about her years running the pattern without bringing to mind the days he spent in relentless pursuit of her. They seemed to go hand in hand. If she missed anything about her trick riding days, it was the rush of landing a stunt and hearing the crowd go wild. But even that didn't compare to the surge of emotions running through her when Jonas would sweep her up in his arms and have his way with her. Back then, he couldn't get enough...kind of the way he couldn't get enough of his dinner right now.

Ava glanced at him, regarding the gratification he displayed while eating. What she wouldn't give to be the pork on his plate.

She grimaced. *Great. Now I'm jealous of a dead pig.*

She pierced the bite-sized piece of meat on her plate and lifted it to her mouth. "I guess there are some things I miss about it," she admitted vaguely. She felt his gaze on her as she chewed.

"So, get back up on that horse."

His movement across the table caught her attention, and she looked up to see him reaching for her. He laid his hand on hers and smiled. "If that's what this is all about, then by all means, don't let me hold you back. I want you to be happy."

Ava shook her head in frustration. *How did he connect the dots between the idea of us being too comfortable with each other and me missing my trick riding days?* "I don't want to go back to trick riding, Jonas. This has nothing to do with that."

He sat back in his chair, buffaloed. "Then what is it?" His eyes narrowed. "Is there someone else?"

She offered a comforting smile. "Of course not. That's absurd." As busy as she was on the ranch, how would she have time for someone else? She barely had time with Jonas. "It's just…"

"For crying out loud, Ava. Just tell me. What the heck does being too comfortable mean?"

He went back to cutting another portion of meat as if he were irritated with the conversation. Getting him to understand what she was talking about without making him feel blame or defensive was what she feared most. This wasn't about finding fault. This was about reconnecting. Rekindling.

As she watched him cut, jab, and shovel his food into his mouth, she realized she should've thought this all through before blurting out her feelings. Even now, after having all day to think about it, she still couldn't put words to her emotions.

"You know what? Let's just forget it." She ate her carrots and shrugged. "It's not important. It's stupid…really."

He stared at her from beneath furrowed brows. "Now, you know as well as I that you can't put a cat back in the bag once you let it out. And this ain't no kitten, darlin'. It's a damn elephant. We've got a five-ton elephant sitting in this room, and you want me to ignore it. But I can't, Ava. I'm a guy. I fix things that need fixing, and I leave them alone if they aren't broken. Obviously, something's broken in our relationship, and it's something I'm doing, else you would've already repaired it yourself. Am I right?"

He didn't wait for her to answer.

"So please, tell me what the hell 'too comfortable' means so I can stop doing it."

Hearing Jonas speak with resentment in his voice made her feel very uncomfortable. She wanted to go back in time before Jonas had asked her why she took so long in the barn. She wanted to clap her hands and go back to the moment when she could've kept the proverbial cat inside the bag and avoided the whole awkward discussion from the get-go with a simple white lie.

"You're tired, Jonas. We can talk about this another time." She wiped the corner of her mouth with a napkin and hoped he'd let it go.

"I work from dawn till dusk. I'm tired every day, Trick. But I'm not too tuckered out to miss the fact that you've got something weighing on your mind." He tossed his napkin next to his plate and stood. He circled the table and knelt beside her, pushing back her chair so she faced him. "I love you, Ava. And I don't want you to want for anything, especially if I can give it to you. Just tell me what you need, and I'll do my best to make it happen." He cradled her face in his hand. "You know I will."

Ava felt reassured of his dedication toward their relationship. It seemed he no more wanted to lose her than she did him. She laid her hand over his, pressing her cheek against the warmth of his palm. His touch was heaven.

"So this 'too comfortable' thing you're worried about... Does it have anything to do with the fact that you and I...haven't...you know?"

She smiled and bit her lip at his insinuation. "A little..."

A small, deep laugh rumbled from his chest as he stroked her cheek. "Or a lot. I'm not stupid, Trick."

Before she could say anything more, he leaned forward and pressed his lips to hers. Her eyes automatically closed with the contact. The heat from his mouth soothed her in ways he could never understand. The tender way his hands threaded through her hair made her feel adored and treasured. She was so glad he thought to kiss her, for it was all she needed. All she wanted from him right now. She needed his undying attention.

Ava slid forward and pressed herself against him, wanting to be as close as possible. In one swift move, he stood and lifted her from the chair. Her heart raced at the notion of Jonas dismissing dinner altogether. It had been over a month since he showed her any kind of intimacy, and she'd begun to think he wasn't attracted to her anymore. She'd always worried their age difference would one day play a role in their relationship, but she didn't want to think it might be after only seven years. Thankfully, those negative, insecure thoughts had left her mind, at least for right now.

"What about dinner?" The pointless question came out of her mouth before she could stop it.

"Forget dinner," he said.

He kicked the bedroom door open, and it banged against the wall before springing back and hitting them. He stumbled, they laughed, and she melted at the sound of his joyous laughter muffled in her kiss.

Chapter Six

As Jonas was about to fling Ava to the bed, it occurred to her that she'd been working all day, sweating, and shoveling manure. The last thing she wanted was to smell like a horse.

"Wait. I need a shower."

He stopped short of the bed and spun around, staggering toward the master bath behind him. "Good idea. I need one too."

"Together?" she suggested.

A manly grunt reverberated in his chest. "Been a while since we've done that."

His kiss deepened as if he were totally on board with the idea. He gripped her shirt, slightly untucking it from her jeans. But she wasn't as patient as her seductive cowboy. She tugged his shirt up over his head and tossed it aside.

The scorching heat of his chest was almost too hot for the summer night they were having, but she didn't care. She clung to him, relishing the feel of his glorious, hard muscles beneath her palms.

With a darkness in his eyes that she hadn't seen in a long time, he set her on her feet and pulled the elastic band from her hair. He watched her long auburn locks fall in messy waves over her shoulders and drank her in with his eyes.

He stepped back just enough to strip off his jeans and boxer briefs. Deep bronze tan lines circled his narrow waist. Washboard abs and muscular thighs took her breath away, but nothing looked as good as the broad muscles of his shoulders and biceps flexing when he reached in to turn on the shower faucet.

"You take too long, Jonas. I don't need foreplay. I just need you."

The tone of her voice surprised her just as much as Jonas obeying her. As he stripped her down to nothing in a matter of seconds, she reveled in the power she had over him.

Not often would Jonas give up his reins, especially when a battle of wills was to be won. Being independent, headstrong, and full of pride was both their curse. They always struggled to retain the upper hand.

Always.

Even after they'd first met, they constantly fought for control. Through the years, she found that even her iron-willed cowboy had weaknesses. And she loved exploiting every one of them for her own personal gain.

Once the last article of clothing was removed, Ava drew Jonas into the hot, steaming water of the shower and regarded her drenched cowboy. His blond hair dripped in dark clumps as droplets of water trailed off his sun-kissed skin. The chiseled edges of his face looked twice as sexy when beads of water danced across them. It amazed her how virile he looked when he was wet.

She squirted a dollop of shampoo in her hard, eager to bathe him from head to toe. It was then she heard the rhythmic vibrating sound of his cell on the tile floor.

"Ignore it," was his response before he sealed his lips over hers. As his hands pulled her tight against him, the pulsing vibrations continued to distract them.

"Who the heck is calling me?" Jonas growled.

His question was rhetorical, but no way would she let him stop and actually look anyway. Eventually, the caller hung up and the disrupting sound ceased. His muscles relaxed, and his determination kicked back in. That is until his cell went into another seizing frenzy.

Jonas sighed exhaustively. "Whoever it is...they sure are persistent."

Ava hung her head, leaning her forehead on his chest. "It's got to be Mr. Corinth."

His expression soured. "I guess I should answer it. I'm sorry baby. This might be an emergency."

He stepped out of the shower and swiped his jeans off the floor. For Mr. Corinth's sake, it better have been urgent enough to interrupt her private time with Jonas. If not, she entertained the idea of pushing the old man down the stairs herself.

"Uh-oh," Jonas muttered as he stared at his cell. "It's not Mr. Corinth. It's Cole."

They looked at each other with concern.

Cole and Jonas had been best friends since kindergarten. All their lives, they were practically inseparable. Besides differing on the schools they attended, the type of girls they dated, and the breeds of horses they preferred, Cole was like blood to Jonas. So it came as no surprise to the people of Meeteetse when Cole bought two-thousand acres directly adjacent to the McKinley family ranch a few years ago. In fact, sixteen hundred of those acres butted up against the west side of Jonas's land, and the two were able to run twice as many cattle across the adjoining farms. They shared a fifty-fifty split of hay, the equipment, and the pastures, but Cole was one-hundred percent bachelor.

Ava called Cole a hermit because he never cared to hang out in public or go into town unless absolutely necessary. The man rarely fraternized in his free time, he scarcely made an effort to date, and he never bothered anyone. Ever.

Yet tonight, he'd called Jonas twice. Something was definitely wrong.

Immediately, she shut off the water and grabbed a towel. "Did he leave a message?"

Jonas shook his head as he punched Cole's speed-dial number. "This can't be good."

Naked and dripping wet, Jonas stared at nothing as he waited for Cole to answer. Ava stepped out of the shower and touched his arm, lending some support. She knew Cole had elderly parents. Maybe something had happened to one of them.

"Hey. Everything all right?" Jonas's gaze flickered toward Ava as he spoke.

"No. It's Sammy. He's hurt. Hurt real bad."

Ava could hear every word Cole said on the other end, and she covered her gaping mouth at the thought of his canine companion sustaining an injury. Given he was an Australian Blue Heeler, a cow kick to the face came with the territory of nipping the heels of cattle on a daily basis. But since Cole was calling about it, it had to be something bigger than a concussion.

"What happened?" Jonas asked.

"Remember that mama grizzly we saw hanging around the outskirts of the ranch? I think she got a little braver."

Jonas tucked his cell between his shoulder and his ear while he pulled on his jeans in a hurry. "How bad is it?"

"He's chewed up pretty good. Back leg's a mess. I called Doc Peterson, and she's on her way."

Ava knew it must have been bad if Jonas didn't bother to dry off or pull on his boxer briefs. He just zipped his jeans, threw on his shirt, and darted for the sock drawer in the other room. She followed on his heels, listening as he dressed on the edge of the bed.

"Are you sure it's a bear attack?"

"I'm not sure of anything," Cole said. "All I know is we have thirty horses and two-hundred head of cattle to worry about. If it's the same grizzly we spotted, she's got two hungry cubs and a smorgasbord of easy pickins. You might want to bring your rifle."

"Right. I'm on my way." Jonas stuffed his cell in his front pocket and headed for the kitchen. He opened the cabinet and snagged a box of ammunition for his .444 lever-action rifle. "Do me a favor, Trick. Call Luke at Wyoming Fish and Wildlife and have him meet me at Cole's. Tell him we have a possible nuisance grizzly."

"Shouldn't we call the game warden?"

"That's Luke's call."

Ava's head spun as she zeroed in on the boxes of high-powered bullets stacked on her kitchen table. "Wait. You're not really going to shoot the bear, are you?"

Jonas didn't even look at her as he stuffed his feet in his boots. "Grizzlies are still on the endangered list, you know that. It's just for our protection."

She didn't have time to process. He righted his Stetson on his head, lifted his weapon from above the kitchen door, and kissed her on the cheek.

"Don't forget to call Luke."

She followed him toward the door, gripping the frame as she watched him sprint off the porch steps toward his truck. She slumped against the screen door, unable to do anything but stand there helpless. Disappointment clung to her like the damp terrycloth hugging her torso.

After looking down and adjusting the towel, she couldn't help but feel an immense pang of anxiety. God knew a large portion of her worried for Cole's dog, given the poor animal had a terrible run-in with a bear, and now the man she loved was running off to track it. But another part of her felt something akin to disenchantment for the magical moment that had been ripped from her hands in the blink of an eye.

At that instant, Ava realized it wasn't so much that she and Jonas were too comfortable with each other. It was that life, all too often, had a way of getting between her and the cowboy she so desperately missed.

Chapter Seven

Jonas sped down the windy backroad toward Cole's ranch in his four-wheel-drive Chevy truck. In reckless pursuit, he turned down the drive, gravel-sliding to a halt in front of the barn next to Doc Peterson's vehicle. He grabbed his rifle from the front seat and slammed the door, running to meet his friend.

When he entered the barn and saw the scene, his heart leapt into his throat. Three horses stood tied and saddled in the aisleway as Cole stared with grave concern at his dog lying in a stall of fresh hay. Copious amounts of blood stained the ground as well as Cole's hands. The vet hovered over the Heeler, administering fluids through an IV in one of its good legs.

Jonas hesitated to ask how the dog was doing for fear of a grim prognosis. Instead, he gave Cole's shoulder a quick squeeze. Together, the two men watched as the skilled vet assessed the gaping wound.

Dr. Charlotte Peterson, or "Charlie" as everyone in

Meeteetse called her, was a beautiful brunette with a killer smile. It wasn't often that she shared it, as her job hardly provided her with an occasion. She dealt mostly with animal sickness and trauma—moments when a toothy grin would be completely inappropriate.

She did, however, retain the respect and admiration from the locals as the best vet in Park County. Many in town spoke of their concern for the young physician and the shoes she'd have to fill in taking over her father's practice. But Charlotte proved them all wrong, including Jonas, who was used to consulting the original Dr. Charlie Peterson and his veterinary service.

"What do you think, Doc?" Cole's voice was low and full of angst.

Dr. Peterson looked up and regarded both men. "He's lucky he got away when he did. Had the bear cut his femoral artery, you'd be burying this animal."

Jonas grimaced at the vet's blunt assessment. He knew the woman wasn't known for her sympathetic bedside manner, but he wished she could've used a little bit more discretion where Cole was concerned. Sammy meant more to Cole than just a working cattle dog.

Jonas glanced at his friend, regarding him carefully. The man looked as if he were in shock. He stood stock-still, his face ashen. Jonas knew Cole needed to hear some strand of good news to help him through this situation. Despite Cole's calm outer display, Jonas bet the man was going through utter hell.

He stepped forward and squatted next to the vet. "So he's going to live, right, Doc?"

"Oh, he'll live. But it's going to be a long haul. Fortunately for him, he's got three other legs to hobble around on." She paused for a moment, listening to his heart with a stethoscope. "Okay, he seems stable enough to move him. I have to take him to the office so I can properly flush this wound and sew him up. He'll have drain tubes and a lampshade around his head until the stitches come out. You boys want to help me load him in the truck?"

"I'll do it," Jonas offered. "But I don't think he's going to like this much."

"I gave him some meds in his IV, so he shouldn't feel too much pain. Since he knows you, how about you take the head in case he does decide to bite?"

"Right." Jonas wanted to laugh at the doc's suggestion, though he knew it was best. Sammy was a cattle dog, loyal to only a handful of people. Jonas was one of them, but that didn't make him feel any better about being so close to the dog's teeth. He handed Cole his rifle and nodded. "I got this. Okay?"

Cole turned and staked the weapon, barrel first, in the saddle holster on the closest horse, but that was it. No words. No thank you. No argument.

Inwardly, Jonas worried more about his friend than the dog. A little medical maintenance would do wonders for Sammy, but what could he possibly do to help Cole?

Shrugging off the urge to comfort him, Jonas bent over Sammy's shoulders and waited for Dr. Peterson to get situated at the hind end. As she clamped the fluid bag between her teeth, Jonas observed the dog's brown eyes. They were glassy and vacant, pitiful as they met his gaze. A small whimper escaped him. "It's all right, boy. Easy, Sam."

On the count of three, Jonas and Doc Peterson lifted the dog and carried him out of the barn. Cole followed without a sound. Once they reached the vet's truck, Cole opened one of the dog carriers strapped in the back of the bed and slid it forward on the tailgate.

"How long before Sammy can come home?" Cole asked, pulling the IV bag from Doc's teeth so she could answer.

"Couple days. Not long. I want to at least keep him overnight for observation. I'll know more tomorrow."

Sammy let out another long whine as they slid him inside and shut the door. Cole put his hand on the carrier and tapped the top. "It's all right, Sam Bone."

Jonas peeked inside the crate through the peepholes. "Don't you worry, Sammy. Doc's gonna fix you up right. You'll be home before you know it." Jonas said those words more for Cole's sake than the dog's, reminding him that his companion was in good hands.

As Dr. Peterson acquired Cole's signature for consent of care, Luke pulled in. Dusk was fast approaching, which meant they had about an hour of daylight to scour the area for the grizzly. Not much time, as far as Jonas was concerned.

"Evening, Luke. Thanks for coming so soon."

Jonas shook hands with Luke Moore, a long-time resident of Meeteetse. He wore the standard red shirt of the Wyoming Fish and Wildlife uniform and a sober expression, proof that Ava had clued him in on the general details.

Jonas also noticed the man carried a high-powered tranquilizer gun. The thought of having to use their weapons, whether rifle or otherwise, gave Jonas a very uneasy feeling. It came with the job of being a cattle rancher in the big country, but he still didn't like it.

"I came as quick as I could," Luke said, looking to both Cole and Dr. Peterson for answers. "Ava said we have a potential grizzly on our hands?"

"Judging by the injury to Cole's dog, it's a bear," Doc

assured with confidence. "Wolves and coyotes use their teeth for kills. These are definitely claw marks."

"You can confirm that?" Luke asked as he stepped forward to shake Cole's hand. Cole held up his bloody palms, indicating a formal handshake was unnecessary.

"I know the routine, Luke," Doc Peterson said. "It'll be in my report by morning." She hopped in her truck and snapped off her latex gloves before shutting the door. "I'll call you first thing tomorrow morning, Cole."

Cole nodded once, and she started the engine, then pulled away.

Like Jonas, Luke noticed the quiet demeanor of the man. Luke and Jonas exchanged glances, knowing the tension in the air was as thick as cold molasses. Luke broke the awkward silence by clearing his throat. "I assume you have a horse for me?"

Jonas answered for Cole, as he seemed to be somewhere else. "Yeah. In the barn. Ready to go."

"Now, you know this isn't cut-and-dry, and we're not taking down a bear tonight. You know the drill. They're protected animals. Your rifles are for your protection only. Got that? We're not on a vengeful hunt here."

Jonas replied that he understood, but Cole didn't.

"Cole?" Luke probed. "You listening?"

Only his gaze shifted toward Luke. "I hear you."

"Do you? 'Cause I know how you feel about that dog. And as bad I feel for what happened tonight, you can't go out there—"

"I said I heard you." Cole turned on a dime and headed toward the barn, alone.

Luke sighed restlessly and looked to Jonas for answers.

Cole was a no-nonsense kind of guy. If he said he understood federal law and wouldn't hunt down the grizzly out of bitter resentment, then Jonas believed him. "He's fine, Luke. He's just dealing the only way he knows how."

As they proceeded toward the barn, Luke made a suggestion. "Maybe it's best if he stays behind."

"You saw his hands, Luke. His dog almost died. Cut him some slack."

"That's the only slack I'm giving him, Jonas. I'm not dealing with a vigilante. My ass could be in a sling if he doesn't follow the law."

"I understand."

"Did you take a head count on the cattle?"

"Not yet."

"Don't you think you should?" Luke stopped abruptly before they entered the barn. "Might be best."

Jonas turned toward Luke and noticed the look of reluctance on the man's face. "All right. I get your drift. Let me talk to Cole. Give me a sec."

Jonas left Luke's side and entered the barn. As he approached, Cole finished washing his hands in a bucket of water.

"We ready?" Cole asked, shaking them off.

"Yeah, we're ready." Jonas looked at the ground, unsure how to proceed. He removed his Stetson and scratched his head.

"What the hell's wrong with you, McKinley? You got something to say? Say it."

Jonas replaced his hat back on his head and sighed. With Cole, short and blunt was always better. "Look, it's getting late and we need a head count on the cattle. You up for that?"

Cole glanced toward Luke, who paced the ground. "He doesn't trust me." Before Jonas could defend Luke, Cole cut him off. "Fine. I'll count the damn steers." In a few quick steps, Cole rounded his horse's hind end and mounted. He gave Jonas a hard look before reining his quarter horse aside. "If you want to find where Sammy was attacked, just follow the blood trail. I'll call you when I get a count."

Cole didn't wait for Jonas's reply. He barreled out of the barn, past Luke, leaving a cloud of dust behind him.

Chapter Eight

Ava rolled over in bed and checked the alarm clock again. Jonas had been gone for over three hours. What was keeping him? Was Sammy worse than they thought? Were they able to track down the bear? Or worse, did the bear find them?

Groaning aloud, she sat up and swung her legs off the side of the bed. She stepped into her slippers and snagged her robe from the back of the door, then made her way through the living room. Thoughts of Jonas wrestling with a grizzly crept into her brain before she could stop them. She hated not knowing what was keeping him and wished he had call her with an update so she didn't have to endure the worst-case scenarios playing out in her mind.

Rubbing her sleepy eyes, she headed toward the kitchen to make some coffee. Maybe a little TV would help tame her wild imagination.

By the time she reached the counter, she heard Jonas's truck pull in the drive. Anxious to see if he was all right, she darted out the door onto the front porch. He circled his truck with slow, heavy steps, his rifle in one hand, his hat in the other. She froze at the portentous look on his face. Her heart sank.

She hesitated to even ask. "How's Sammy?"

Jonas climbed the three stairs and handed her his hat. "He's all right. He's sliced up good, but he'll recover."

"The cattle?"

"They're all accounted for according to Cole. But we've got bigger problems now."

To Ava's keen perception, Jonas looked more exhausted than worried. It wasn't often anything could ruffle his feathers. Whatever the issue, it was larger than just a simple bear encounter.

Ava reached out and touched his arm. "What's wrong?"

"I hate to say this to you, but it looks like we're going to have to cancel trail riding for the entire week. Maybe even next week's too. How many you got on the schedule?"

Ava brought to mind the calendar on her desk, adding up the number of names she'd added over the last six months. "I'm not sure of the exact numbers, but it's at least thirty to forty a day. Maybe more on the weekend."

Jonas sighed and pinched the bridge of his nose. "That's a lot of calls. A lot of money too. But it has to be done. We have no choice until we can pinpoint the bear's whereabouts and prove to Fish and Wildlife that she's a nuisance bear so they can relocate her."

Ava understood his frustration and the fact that this predicament was not an easy fix. Bears often traveled many miles in a day in search of food, not to mention they were elusive as well. Sometimes they lingered in an area and sometimes they didn't. The only thing that could be done tonight was make sure that tomorrow's clients were notified before morning. She recalled the time of night and dreaded the amount of time it would take to get through the list.

She reached for his rifle and ushered Jonas inside. "Why don't you get your shower, and I'll start making calls."

Jonas nodded in silence and toed off his boots at the door. As he headed toward the bedroom, she watched him unbutton his shirt and slip it off his shoulders. His muscular bare back caught her eye. As much as she wanted to join him, she knew getting a head start on the calls would make more sense.

She leaned his gun by the door and hung his hat on the hook. The squeal of the squeaky bathroom faucet and the sound of running water caused her heart to ache again as she remembered how their spontaneous intimate evening had been cut short. If not for this terrible turn of events, she would've liked to have rekindled that fire her cowboy had started during dinner.

Instead, she pulled his plate from the fridge and

popped it in the microwave. As the nuker hummed in the background, she collected the client files from her office and returned to the kitchen table to make the first call.

As she expected, a tired female voice answered the phone. "H-hello?"

"Mrs. Baker?"

"Yes…this is she."

"I'm sorry to call at such a late hour, ma'am. This is Ava from the McKinley Ranch and Riding Stables."

"Okay…" she said, confusion lacing her voice. "May I ask what this is in regards to?"

Ava heard a grumpy man's voice in the background demanding to know who was calling her cell, followed by a muffled conversation. "It's the riding stables."

"What the hell do they want? It's eleven o'clock at night, for crying out loud! We've got kids sleeping in this hotel room."

Ava tried to interject. "Ma'am? Mrs. Baker?"

"Yes, I'm here."

"My apologies for waking your family, but I needed to get a hold of you. We've had a bear sighting near the trails this evening, and unfortunately, we're going to have to cancel all horseback riding for this week. I'm trying to reach you tonight so you don't make a trip for nothing in the morning. I'm so very sorry for any inconvenience this may cause you and your family. I assume you're here on vacation?"

"We are."

"Again, I apologize for the inconvenience. Rest assured the credit card we have on hold for the ride will not be charged."

"Okay, thank you."

Ava heard Mrs. Baker whispering as she filled her husband in on the situation. A moment later, she added, "Um…my husband wants to know if there are other stables around Meeteetse that would be open for business. To be honest, our children were looking forward to riding horses on their vacation. I feel bad asking for your competitor's contact info, but I don't want to disappoint the kids."

"I totally understand," Ava replied, remembering her days of taking small vacation trips with her son. "I don't mind at all. It's your vacation. No one should be disappointed. Do you have a pen handy?"

Ava felt a hand on her shoulder, and she turned to see Jonas reaching for a stack of client files on the table. He leaned against her back in nothing but a towel, only making eye contact with her as he snagged his share of client names. Without so much as a good-bye, he strolled back toward the bedroom to make his calls.

Ava ogled him from head to toe as he retreated from

the room. His short blond hair was dark with dampness. The tight little orbs of his butt filled out the towel he wore around his waist. The muscles of his calves flexed with each step he took. And the wide expanse of his bare shoulders and back filled her mind with thoughts of her nails clawing down them. He was about as sexy as a man could get. For a few breath-stealing seconds, she almost forgot she was on the phone.

"Are you still there?" Mrs. Baker asked.

"Oh yeah. Yeah. Sorry," Ava stuttered as she fought to remember why she was waiting on the line in the first place.

"I've got a pen. Go ahead with the first name," Mrs. Baker whispered.

Ava's memory came back, and she rattled off a couple of names and numbers from some of the other local riding stables she was familiar with, her thoughts still on the half-naked cowboy in the next room. In her struggle to maintain focus on Mrs. Baker and their future vacation plans, she luckily had enough presence of mind to encourage the Bakers to drop the McKinley name when scheduling another ride. Being a small town, almost everyone who resided in Meeteetse felt the need to oblige other businesses, especially when the callers came with a recommendation. It was common sense to essentially "spread the wealth," given many vacationers frequented more than one stable a week in order to soak up as much of the Wild West as they could before heading back to their ordinary lives.

After Ava ended the call, she glanced over her shoulder toward the bedroom and revisited the image of Jonas in his towel. She wondered if he still sported the terrycloth around his waist as he talked on the phone. Or, better yet, if he'd finished his calls and slipped naked beneath the covers of the bed.

Curious to know either way, she left the table to check. As she peered into the bedroom, she found him sitting up in bed—the covers pulled to his waist—with his eyes closed. His cell phone lay in his upturned hand and a stack of opened folders lay beside him. It looked as though he hadn't made it through one call before he passed out from exhaustion.

Ava smiled with pity for Jonas and sat on the edge of the bed next to him. She gathered his cell and the files and laid them on the end table beside the bed. She reached out and touched his arm, stroking the fine hairs along his long, muscular forearm. For a few splendid moments, she admired every beautiful inch of him as he slept, until she herself yawned with fatigue.

What she wouldn't give to curl up next to this gorgeous man and sleep.

Knowing she had a responsibility to contact the mountain of names on Monday's ride schedule, Ava ignored the temptation to curl up next to him and stood. She rolled him on his side and adjusted the covers over his body. He mumbled a slur of words but didn't wake up. She turned out the lamp and grabbed the files before tiptoeing toward the door. With her hand on the knob, she glanced back at him one last time. Silently, she sent up a prayer of thanks for keeping her cowboy out of harm's way.

While she should've been grateful that he lay in bed, safe and sound, she couldn't help but feel disappointed that he'd forgotten about the little spark of passion they had shared. It sure as heck hadn't slipped her mind. She could still feel him on her skin. The scorch of his lips burned in her memory like a blazing campfire on a cool summer's night.

Maybe that was the problem with their relationship. Maybe she was more into him than he was her. She'd been in that kind of relationship before, and it hurt once she recognized the signs.

Was their dry spell a sign?

The thought of Jonas growing disinterested wasn't far-fetched given his age, and it wasn't implausible for a man like Jonas to become bored with having an older woman.

A strange sadness sank in, and her heart tore in two.

She hated the thought of Jonas losing interest in her. He was such a gentleman, though, that even if he were falling out of love, she didn't think he'd admit it. Or worse, he didn't even know he was falling out of love. In fact, he'd seemed completely blindsided by her concern about being too comfortable when she'd brought it up.

Maybe he wasn't losing interest in her. Maybe he was just so contented with her in his life that she'd grown to be more like a close friend than a lover.

No matter the issue, she wasn't going down without a fight. Tomorrow, she'd change how she presented herself to Jonas. No more going through the motions as Ava, the loyal confidante. Come morning, this old mare would be Ava, the sexy little filly.

Chapter Nine

Ava awoke to the sound of muffled voices outside. She stretched and realized she wasn't in bed, but on the living room couch. She opened her eyes and looked around. She'd been draped with her favorite blanket, while her cell and files sat neatly piled on the coffee table in front of her. Next to that sat a steaming cup of coffee and a note from Jonas.

Discerning that she must have fallen asleep as she made the last of Monday's cancellations, she bolted upright and snatched the paper of scribbled names she'd made. A sigh of relief escaped her when she saw a line through each one.

Leaning back on the couch in relief, she plucked the note from the table. The sight of Jonas's handwriting made her smile. Though it resembled chicken scratch, she loved that he took the time to write her a message.

I know you think we're getting too comfortable with each other, but for the record, I wasn't the least bit comfortable sleeping without you. Whether you think so or not, I need you by my side.

Hope the coffee's still hot.
J

She glanced at the steam rising from the brim and reached for the mug as she stood, her heart melting over his words. Holding the cup in both hands, with Jonas's little note nestled between her knuckles, she walked toward the window in hopes of catching a glimpse of her considerate cowboy—the man who claimed he *needed* her.

Warm sunshine greeted her through the pane at the same moment she saw Jonas's handsome face. He stood in front of seven employees, his hands loosely crossed at his back as he talked. A five-o'clock shadow darkened his jaw. He looked tired, and his shoulders drooped. She couldn't hear a lick, but judging by the somber faces and stiff postures of the workers, it was obvious Jonas was filling them in on the unfortunate incident with Cole's dog and what would happen in the days to follow.

They hadn't really talked about it, but she knew Jonas wouldn't lay off any of the staff. Despite the trail tours being on hold, there was always plenty of work to be done on the ranch to keep them on the clock. Four of the female employees were college-aged gals who needed a steady income to pay their tuitions for the upcoming semester, and Rhonda was a single mother of two who needed this job most of all.

As for the two hired hands, Rod and Brody Galven, they, too were dependent on their income, as they'd been on the McKinley ranch since they were teens. This job was all they knew. Come right down to it, every one of the staff was dedicated to the ranch, and Jonas always took care of those who were loyal to him.

The only two missing from the group were Cole and his dog. Even Sammy was an asset to the ranch, working hard to help the guys round up cattle for vaccinations and pasture rotation. She wondered if Sammy's injury would keep him from doing what he loved.

As Ava watched the staff disperse and Jonas pull out his cell, she decided it was high time to get to work as well. She not only had horses to feed and stalls to muck, she needed to get her butt in gear working on Jonas's heartstrings.

As she made her way to the bedroom, she flipped his note and read it once more. There was a sense of undeniable resolve in his words that she fancied. She was also pleased he wasn't *comfortable* sleeping without her. His disapproval with that alone made her feel more desirable, and she clung to the hope that he'd never be comfortable doing it.

To her, this was progress. At least he could admit he needed her. He'd put it in writing, for goodness sake. The question was why?

Was it because he loved her so much he couldn't live without her? Or because he couldn't sustain the McKinley ranch without her help?

Just as she'd decided last night, she wasn't going to succumb to being just his friend or another hired hand. She would make him realize that she could be so much more if he only took the time to notice.

To put her plan in motion, she needed to dress appropriately for the occasion. Men were simple beings. They didn't need much more than a tempting visual to get their hearts racing. Jonas more than proved that when they'd first met. And it was his persistence that had caused her to cave. All she needed to do was bring him back to that way of thinking, and nothing said *Come and get it* like a tight pair of jeans.

She set her coffee mug on the dresser and ripped open the drawer. She found the tightest pair of jeans she owned and held them up. For a second, she doubted she'd be able to squeeze into them again. She took a gander at herself in the mirror and bit her lip. She swiveled at the hips to get a better look at her rear, debating the possibility.

In her trick riding days, she had a muscular frame with a tiny waist. Ten years later, she was still strong because of the daily farmwork but admittedly a little thick in the middle. The one thing that hadn't changed over the years was her ample cup size. For that, she was thankful. Given the right amount of support and padding, she imagined she could still stop traffic with those babies.

Ava smiled with pride and ditched the denim for a pretty, black lace push-up bra. Gathering her bravado, along with a button-down plaid shirt and more comfortable jeans, she dressed in a flash.

While brushing her teeth, she contemplated leaving her hair down. Jonas always liked when her hair fell in cascading waves around her shoulders, but she thought otherwise. She didn't want to come off too strong or too obvious. She only wanted her cowboy's attention, not Rod's or Brody's.

With her hair in the usual ponytail, a dab of gloss on her lips, and a provocative strip of cleavage bursting from her shirt, she was ready to strut her stuff. At the door, she slipped on her boots, her heart racing as she scanned the back lot for Jonas. Though he was nowhere to be seen, she couldn't help but imagine his surprise when he laid eyes on her.

Pushing open the door, she caught sight of the two brothers, each carrying buckets of grain to the cattle lot. Her boots thudded against the wood porch floor, announcing her approach. Rod tripped on way through the gate as he did a double take at her sexy getup, and Brody almost rammed into his brother's back.

Inwardly, she smiled and squared her shoulders. "Morning, boys."

Rod tried hard not to stare and cleared his throat. "Morning, ma'am."

Brody nodded once and glanced around as if looking for Jonas. He seemed uneasy with the fact that his boss's girlfriend appealed to his senses, and that Jonas might catch wind of it.

Ava pretended not to notice as she rested her elbows on top of the fence and watched them pour their buckets in the feeders. "You guys know where Jonas is?"

Again, Rod was the only man who possessed a tongue for speaking. "I think he's in the barn saddling up. Said something about moving cattle today on account of that bear."

She tapped the top fence rung and thanked them before heading to the barn. During her casual stroll, she felt Rod's and Brody's gazes on her backside as sure as the sun was hot. She swore she even heard the words *hot damn* escape Rod's mouth, a comment not meant for her ears. Little did he know she needed that small token of encouragement to face Jonas. If not for their rousing reaction, she might have thought twice about her plan and run back inside to change her clothes.

Tamping down her nerves, she entered the barn and searched for her cowboy. Winchester stood tied in the aisleway, head down and saddled up. Madeline and Jolee mucked stalls, while the other two, Addison and Hayden, scooped grain into rubber feeder pails. Rhonda, who led another horse inside, stopped dead in her tracks.

"Well, look at you, Miss Ava. You got a hot date?"

Ava shushed her friend. "No, nothing like that." She peered throughout the barn again for Jonas. "I'm just trying to get Jonas's attention."

Rhonda scoffed and tied the horse next to Winchester. "Oh, I'm certain you'll grab it dressed like that. What's the occasion?"

Ava's bubble burst, and she rolled her eyes, realizing how ridiculous she must look dressed like a hustling buckle bunny. "There's no occasion, really. I'm just..." Words to explain her motivation for such an outfit failed her in the presence of another female. "I'm just an idiot."

Rhonda leaned closer. "No woman is an idiot for trying to look good for her man. It's just a shame that men don't realize what they have already and force us to resort to shit like this to remind them."

"You're right. I need to get out of these clothes."

Rhonda grabbed Ava by the arm. "That's not what I meant. You went to this much trouble to get all dolled up. You keep rockin' it. I just didn't peg Jonas as a blind man."

Ava frowned. "He's not blind. I know he knows what he's got, but he doesn't seem to show it as often as he used to. We've been together too long, I suppose."

"Hey now," Rhonda corrected her. "That's no excuse, and you shouldn't accept that. I may be divorced, but it doesn't mean I didn't give my all to save my marriage. Believe me, I tried. But it's a two-way street in any relationship. You can't be the only one who's willing to work at it. He's got to know that just because you're committed, doesn't give him the right to forget how to treat you. We need to know how much they love us, and more importantly, they need to show us. Am I right? I know I'm right. And you, Miss Ava, shouldn't sell yourself short."

"I suppose." Standing between the two horses, shielded from everyone's view, Ava still couldn't help but feel vulnerable. In the blink of an eye, she went from confident to cowardly waiting on Jonas. She wasn't cut out for this seduction crap.

Rhonda lifted Ava's chin with a kind hand. "Chin up.

You can do this."

Ava sighed. "How? What the heck do I do? What do I say to him?"

Rhonda chuckled. "You don't have to say a thing. These girls are doing all the work for you," she said, pointing at Ava's chest. "Just go about your business as usual. Trust me. He'll notice."

Jonas's voice echoed through the barn walls as he came walking in with a saddle draped over his shoulder, a pad under his arm, and a cell to his ear. "Nah, we got this, Cole. You take care of Sammy. I'm just glad he's doing all right."

"Here," Rhonda whispered, shoving a pair of grooming tools in Ava's hands. "Act natural and brush this horse. Drop a currycomb or something when he comes around."

"What?"

"Do it," Rhonda insisted as she slipped away. "Drop it and bend over."

Chapter Ten

With a metal currycomb in her right hand and a soft bristle brush in her left, Ava groomed the horse, trying to feign a sense of business as she waited for Jonas. She trembled as she prepped the horse Jonas would saddle next. Her heart skipped with each long stroke across the horse's back and belly, worrying she'd look more like a fool than a sexy filly.

"Well, hey," he said in surprise. "I didn't know you were awake. I thought Rhonda was helping me."

Ava kept her back to Jonas and conversed with him as she'd done many times before. "She is. She's getting a horse for Brody. I think." Only trouble was, every sentence came out stiff and choppy, almost robotic in nature. She panicked and looked for Rhonda for reassurance, finding her tucked within the nearest stall. Rhonda nodded and urged Ava on, mouthing the words, *Drop the comb.*

"I guess you heard me on the phone with Cole, then, huh?" Jonas said from behind her. "He said Sammy's doing good. Doc stitched him up, and he's hobbling around like it's nothing."

Ava prepared herself for the bend-over routine. She squeezed her eyes shut, hardly ready. "Does that mean he can come home today?"

"As far as I know. Cole's on his way to Doc's right now." Within a two-breath lapse, Jonas piped up again. "Are you about finished with that horse, Trick? I got shit to do. Come on, move that ass."

A hard swat landed on her bottom, something she hadn't expected. He had startled her so badly, the comb fell from her grasp without her faking it. She shuffled her feet and met Rhonda's gaze with wide eyes.

Bend over, Rhonda mouthed.

With an awkward stoop, Ava bent over to pick up the comb from under the horse. Her rear bumped into Jonas's thigh, and he stumbled sideways into Winchester's side. The pad he had in his possession hit the ground, and Winchester snorted from the slight commotion but settled quickly, licking his lips.

"What's wrong with you, Trick?" Jonas jibed. "You're awful jumpy this morning."

Full of embarrassment, Ava turned around to face him and apologize, but Jonas was bent over picking up the pad. As soon as he stood, his gaze immediately dropped to her bosom. His eyes widened in surprise and a half smile twitched at his lips as he looked her up and down.

"Well, hello, darlin'. Whatcha got going on here?"

Ava swallowed, unsure of how to reply. She tried to remember her college days of flirting, but they seemed so long ago. She faked innocence and leaned against the horse, draping her arm over its back. "I don't know what you mean, McKinley."

A laugh escaped Jonas, and his dimples popped into place. "The way you're dressed. What's with the...the..."

"Cleavage, Jonas," Ava answered for him. "It's called cleavage. I've always had it."

"Indeed you have." Jonas took off his hat and scratched his neck. His gaze shifted from her eyes to her chest and back again. He didn't seem to know where to look.

While his uneasiness should've amused Ava, it actually disappointed her. In their earlier years, he would've stared without shame or remorse. He might have even taken one breast in his grasp. Now, he only looked uncomfortable.

She tried to give him the benefit of the doubt, as there were others in the barn who could see them interacting. She looked for herself, but no one paid a bit of attention to them—except maybe Rhonda.

Ava tried her best to entice him in hopes he'd relax a

little. She stepped forward and drew light circles on his chest. "What's wrong? Don't you like what you see?"

Jonas cleared his throat as Rod had done. "I do." He snickered. "But I have cattle to move. With Cole absent and Sammy hurt, I have a long day ahead of me. There's just the three of us. Unless, of course, you'd like to help."

Ava backed away. "Help? With the cattle?" She mulled over the image of her rounding up and cutting cattle dressed as she was. "I guess I could."

"You guess?"

"Well, I mean I do have all those cancelations I need to take care of for the week and—"

"I'll do them," Rhonda announced, walking out of the stall. "I can make all those calls for you, Miss Ava. You go ahead and help Mr. McKinley, here. I think he needs your help more than anyone else does. Isn't that right?"

Jonas cocked his head as if he were still trying to figure out where Rhonda had come from.

"Mr. McKinley?" Rhonda prompted.

"Right. Yes." He looked back at Ava, the urge to glance southward apparent on his face. "Yes. I could really use your help. Wanna saddle up?"

Ava sighed. "Sure."

Jonas stole one quick glance at her cleavage and shoved the saddle pad at her chest as if to shield her near-naked appearance. He then swung the saddle from his shoulder to the ground, standing it upright. "I'll get you a horse." In the blink of an eye, he spun and strode out of the barn.

Ava flipped the pad on the horse's back and glared at Rhonda. "See? He's not the same guy anymore."

"Sure he is," Rhonda said, rounding the horse's rear.

"You saw him. That was not a turned-on man."

Rhonda touched her arm. "Honey, the poor guy's shell-shocked. He doesn't know what to think."

Ava ignored her and threw the saddle up on the horse, then cinched the girth. "I need to go change. I can't run cattle in this push-up bra."

"The hell you can't. You leave it on, and this time, be a little more seductive."

Ava plopped her hands on her hips. "Are you out of your mind? Rod and Brody are going to be with us. I can't be seductive with them around."

"All the more reason," Rhonda contended. "In fact, Rod and Brody are bound to help your cause. You know how it is when other men happen to take notice of a man's woman. Jonas'll go out of his mind with jealousy."

"I'm not trying to make him jealous, Rhonda. I just want him to desire me."

"Then go out there and flaunt what you want him to

have. And right under Rod's and Brody's noses if you have to." Rhonda chuckled as she continued. "Darlin', you'll have him so worked up, he'll probably drag you off that horse and take you right there in the woods."

Ava reached up and gave the saddle horn a hard shove, centering it. "I don't know if I can do this."

"Look," Rhonda said, softening her voice. "You're a beautiful woman, with or without that push-up. But if you want to get this man's attention, you're going to have to dangle the bait a little bit more."

"I don't know if you've noticed or not, but at my age, my bait already dangles."

"Oh, shut up, it does not. When you've had two kids and breastfed them both, then you can claim that. Now, here's what you do. After you're saddled up, walk the horses out to the trough and dab a little water on your neck so it runs down your shirt. Lean forward if you have to, but make sure he sees that water trail on your skin. Men love that stuff, women hot and sweaty, even if they're just faking it."

Ava stared at her friend in disbelief. "You've been watching Fifty Shades again, haven't you?"

"Hey, I have needs too, you know." Rhonda's eyes lit up, and she shushed Ava before she could comment further. "Here he comes. Remember what I told you.

Dangle it. Trust me, it's as easy as fishing."

Ava's jaw clenched at the thought of trying to dangle anything. At this rate, she figured she'd only alarm Jonas rather than appeal to him. Taking a deep breath, she faced Jonas with a smile as he led two more horses into the barn.

Without a word, she accepted the lead rope he handed her and began saddling her horse while Jonas saddled the other. Rhonda sidled up next to her and pretended nothing was out of the ordinary.

"Miss Ava, where are the files so I can make those calls for you?"

"They're in my office, on the desk. Today's files are on the coffee table. So, if you have time, you can file those back when you're finished. If you don't mind, that is."

"I don't mind at all." Rhonda winked and whispered before she left, "Dangle."

Ava shook her head and finished fitting the bit into her horse's mouth. As she secured the throat latch, she wondered what was going through Jonas's mind. Did he enjoy the sight of her dressed in such a provocative manner? Or was he irritated by it?

"You ready?" Jonas asked.

"Yeah."

Rhonda's words echoed in her brain. *Dangle it.*

"Let's go, boys!" Jonas shouted to Rod and Brody as

he swung up on his horse.

Ava cringed. She pressed herself against Ranger's shoulder as the brothers strolled up, hoping to hide any covert glances they might make in her direction. They stacked their empty buckets next to the grain bin and mounted up next to Jonas.

"What's with the fourth horse?" Rod asked.

"Ava's coming with us," Jonas stated dryly.

"That's a nice change," Rod replied.

Ava caught the sideways glare Jonas gave Rod. Maybe Rhonda was right. Maybe having other men present would spur Jonas into being the alpha male she always knew him to be. She hid her grin and walked her horse out of the barn toward the trough, just as Rhonda instructed. The three guys followed, silent as they trotted behind her.

As Ranger lowered his head to drink, Winchester took his place next to her. Jonas said nothing as he fiddled with his reins and readjusted his hat. Ava waited a few moments more before she made her move.

Standing between the horses, she fanned herself. "Looks like it's going to be another hot one."

Jonas stared out into the field. "Yep."

Ava tried again. "Do you have a handkerchief?"

She saw the skin between his brows pucker, but he didn't question her motives. He pulled it from his back pocket and handed it over. Ava accepted it and dipped it in the trough.

"Sakes alive, it's hot," she said again, drawing out her voice into a soft purr. She then tipped her chin up, opened her shirt slightly, and wrung the kerchief close to her neck. Cold water splashed against her bare skin and dribbled down between her breasts.

Leather squeaked as Jonas shifted in his saddle. She looked up at him, and he immediately averted his gaze. Though he played it cool, he was anything but. Ava smiled and pressed on. This time, she wiped the wet kerchief across her chest in slow strokes and up the column of her neck. She moaned ever so quietly at the relief the cold water gave her.

Jonas grunted like a caveman. "Ava."

"Yes, McKinley?"

Pouring it on thick, she reached back and took hold of the brim of the trough. By arching her back, she offered a clear view of her cleavage, but unfortunately lost her grip and fell right into the water.

Chapter Eleven

Ava jolted upright, gasping and coughing. Clutching the sides of the trough, she thrashed about, trying to hoist herself free. By the time her feet touched the ground, Jonas had already dismounted and was pulling her the rest of the way out. Her tight-fitting clothes now clung to her body like a second skin, and her hair was a soaked, matted mess.

"Are you all right?"

Mortified, she pushed out of Jonas's grasp. "Of course, I'm all right. It's just water."

Jonas wiped his growing smile from his lips, laughter clearly threatening to burst from his chest. "Were you so hot that you had to completely submerge yourself?"

"Seriously? You think I did this on purpose?"

"Trick, I don't know what to think. You've been acting as peculiar as socks on a rooster all morning. What the heck's gotten into you?"

Wringing out the hem of her shirt, she glared at Rod and Brody, who were laughing.

Jonas whipped his head around at the brothers and did the same. "Knock it off, fellas." As they quieted down, Jonas turned back to Ava. "Did you hurt yourself?"

"No!" *Yes, my pride!*

"What's going on with you?" he asked. "Why are you acting like this? Dressing like this?"

Ava groaned aloud. "I don't know. I was just trying to dangle it."

Jonas drew back. "Dangle it?"

If he was confused before, he looked totally befuddled now.

"What the hell are you talking about? Dangle what?"

"Just forget it," Ava growled. "I'm done. I'm freakin' done."

Jonas reached for her, but she dodged his help. "Leave me be. Please."

He stretched out his hands as she stormed toward the house. "Where are you going?"

"To change!" she shouted over her shoulder. "What do *you* think?"

Hot tears welled up in her eyes as she felt the weighty stares of each man. She'd never been so humiliated in her life, and all she wanted to do was crawl in a hole. *No, scream.* Scream bloody murder, then crawl in a hole—right after she murdered Rhonda.

****

Jonas dropped his arms, letting them slap against his legs. "What the hell just happened?"

"Well, from where I was sitting," Rod said, crossing his wrists on the horn of his saddle, "I reckon she was trying her best to catch your eye. And she was doing a damn good job of it...till she slipped and fell in the trough."

Jonas shot Rod a look to kill.

"Hey. You asked, hoss."

Jonas took off his hat and swiped the perspiration from his brow, pondering Rod's assessment. In all honesty, she *had* caught his eye. On several occasions that morning. But why? They had a long list of work to do, and trying to stir up a man's hormones before any of it was done seemed a complete waste of time. What was he supposed to do if his hormones *were* stirred up? Tell Rod and Brody to go on without him? *Right.*

No matter how many times he mulled over the scenarios, he still couldn't figure out Ava's intention. It wasn't like her to flaunt her curves for the world to see. Heck, it wasn't like her to show *any* part of her well-toned body. Even in her trick riding days when she sported the spandex that left little to the imagination, she did so only out of necessity. Loose clothing presented a dangerous risk to the riders who vaulted, spun, and suspended their bodies off the side of a sprinting horse.

Jonas often recalled how much she hated wearing the tight-fitting jumpsuits and how bad she itched to get back into a T-shirt and jeans as soon as her routine was over. If it weren't for the rodeo fans lining up for autographs and pictures, she would've changed the second she left the arena.

Ava had always been a modest girl. Which was why none of this made sense to him. Only with his encouragement had she finally ventured out of her shell. He practically had to move mountains when they first met to get her to believe he wanted more from her than just sex.

He smiled to himself, remembering the first time he'd kissed her in the horse barn at the Cheyenne Frontier Days Rodeo. Despite her objections to have coffee with him, he was able to change her mind with just a little game of domination and seduction.

Though the days of sneaking kisses at every turn had passed, sex with Ava was better now. He didn't have to leap hurdles or spend a bunch of money to prove he loved her. They'd made a life for themselves, working the ranch and living under one roof. They split expenses fifty-fifty and shared the profits as normal couples do. Without a legal document stating marriage, they were still as good as hitched.

So, why the sudden theatrics to gain his attention? Why the talk about being too comfortable? Was she going through a midlife crisis?

As far as he was concerned, she had had his attention from the moment he laid eyes on her. And if she only stopped to notice, she'd realize he *still* had eyes for her. He didn't always have the time to show her because of his responsibilities with the ranch, but he sure as heck wanted to. Left up to him, he'd make love to her every day—especially when she came riding in from a trail tour. Nothing looked hotter to him than a woman in chaps riding a quarter horse.

"Hey, McKinley," Rod called, interrupting his private thoughts. "You want us to ride on? Give you some privacy with the missus for a little bit? She looked pretty upset. Almost as mad as ol' Brody here gets on occasion."

"Shut your hole, Rod," Brody said as he flicked a piece of hay from his horse's mane.

Jonas righted his Stetson on his head and bent to fish his handkerchief out of the trough. As he held the dripping-wet material in his fist, an image of Ava flashed in his mind. His mouth watered just thinking how sexy it was to see her wring water down her shirt. How sweetly her breasts, all plump and pushed up, glistened with water in the sunlight. How supple her lips looked when she tipped her head back. What he wouldn't give to crush those lips in a kiss.

The notion tempted him. He could even feel other parts of his body responding to the idea. But as he contemplated Rod's suggestion, he knew she was beyond mad for making a spectacle of herself. He came to the conclusion that he'd best leave her alone.

"She'll be out soon enough," Jonas said, glancing back at the house. "She might be a woman, but she's no prima donna."

Minutes ticked by as the three of them waited for Ava to return. As he stood there under the hot morning sun, he wondered if she would man up and get her ass out here or if he'd eventually have to go in after her. The more time passed, the more Jonas wasn't so keen on entering that lion's den. He already had a mean mama grizzly to contend with.

"So, speaking of women," Jonas said, breaking the silence. "How's your lady friend, Brody? I haven't heard much about Olivia since she left for Nashville a few weeks ago."

Rod broke into a hearty laugh. "Brody can't admit it yet, but Olivia's gonna be a big star now, and he'll be the last thing she thinks of."

"I don't know about that," Jonas said, lending Brody support. "She's a sweet girl. And loyal too. She's not gonna forget who loves her and who's always been there for her. Her roots run too deep in Meeteetse. Don't you worry, Brody. She'll be back." Jonas winked.

"Well, if she does come back," Rod contended, "it won't be to stay. Mark my words, Olivia's a bird with wings now."

"What do you know about Liv? About *any* woman?" Brody said, smirking.

Rod chuckled and readjusted his bottom in the saddle. "I know enough not to get involved with a gal whose one dream is to get the heck away from small town life. Trust me, you both are wrong. Olivia's as good as gone."

Brody exchanged a look with Jonas, and fashioned his lips in a nervous grin. "I'd like to think you don't know everything, brother."

While the two brothers continued to debate Olivia's future, Jonas's cell buzzed. He took it out and saw that the caller was Cole. "Hey, buddy. How's Sammy doing?"

"Get your ass over here. The bear's back."

"What?"

"You heard me. She's back. I just pulled in the drive with Sammy and caught a glimpse of her and her two cubs. She's hanging around where she got a hold of him yesterday, and the cattle are stirring."

"All right, we'll be there in a few. Call Luke."

"You call Luke, McKinley. I've got cattle to worry about."

"Cole... Don't do anything stupid. You can't shoot her out of spite, and you know it."

"Then you better get your ass over here, 'cause if she so much as tries to take down one of our steers—"

"Cole, I'm serious. Let Luke handle this." Jonas pleaded with his friend, but Cole didn't concede. "Cole. Cole!" When it was obvious Cole had hung up, Jonas cursed and kicked the dirt. Cole's hardheadedness was the one thing that drove him crazy, and he worried this time it might get him thrown in jail, or worse, killed by the grizzly. He fisted his cell, wanting to throw it across the yard.

"Boss?" Brody gently probed.

Jonas pinched his nose. "Brody, hook up the trailer to my truck. Rod, you head over to Cole's. Keep him from doing anything rash until Luke gets there. Brody and I'll trailer the horses over so we can get those cattle moved to safer pasture. You got a gun?"

"On the rack in my truck, as always."

"I don't think you'll need it, but just be safe, you hear?"

"Yes, sir," Rod said, dismounting.

Jonas took off running for the house to inform Ava and dialed Luke's number on the way.

Chapter Twelve

Ava stood in the doorway of her office long enough to catch Rhonda's attention. "See what happens when a forty-year-old woman tries to dangle the bait?"

Rhonda's eyes widened, and she dropped her pen. "Hell's fire, Miss Ava, what happened?"

Ava stomped down the hall toward her bedroom, Rhonda close behind. "I dangled the bait, just like you said, and fell in the trough, that's what happened. I thought you said it was as easy as fishing."

"Well, honey, when I said fishing...I didn't mean literally."

Ava unbuttoned her shirt and ripped the drenched fabric from her body. "I told you I couldn't do this. And to make matters worse, Rod and Brody were there to see it. I looked like an idiot."

"Aw, now, I'm sure it wasn't that bad."

Ava glared at Rhonda, her stringy wet hair clinging to her neck and face. "Look at me. I'm a drowned rat. There's nothing sexy about this."

Rhonda looked Ava up and down. "I'm sure if we asked the guys to weigh in right now, they'd disagree."

Ava looked down at herself and realized she was standing there in nothing but a push-up bra and jeans. "That's not what I mean."

Rhonda dismissed Ava's anger with a wave of her hand. "I know exactly what you mean and I think you're being too critical of yourself. Now, you just get out of those wet clothes, slap on another push-up bra, and march your butt back out there. You've got a man to seduce."

Before Ava could contest Rhonda's orders, Jonas burst through the door. He stopped dead in his tracks and blinked repeatedly, as if stunned.

Ava's frustration climbed. "I told you I'm coming. I just have to change my clothes."

"Don't bother," Jonas spat. "I mean…you *should*…put on clothes."

Ava slapped her hands on her hips. "And why's that?"

The minute her question blurted from her mouth, she realized it sounded utterly ridiculous. *'Cause you can't round up cattle with Rod and Brody in your bra.*

Jonas's lips puckered. "W-What?" He stuttered for a few seconds and shook his head as if to clear it. "Dammit, I don't have time." He glanced beside him and grabbed the rifle that was leaning against the wall in the corner. "The grizzly's back at Cole's—"

Ava gasped. "Again? I'm coming with you."

"No, it's too dangerous. I need you and the girls to round up the horses and get them back in their stalls. Until the bears are trapped and relocated, we're putting Cole's cattle in the horse lot."

"But Jonas—"

"Ava, don't argue with me." Jonas turned to dash out the door but stopped short and gawked at her one last time. He cleared his throat in a very subtle way and then left, tripping out onto the porch.

"Oh my gosh. I can't believe this."

"I know," Rhonda agreed. "Jonas was practically drooling over you."

"What? No. I'm talking about the bear."

"Oh. Right." Rhonda altered her expression to one of concern. "The bear." Then she grinned from ear to ear. "But did you see how Jonas looked at you?"

Ava sighed. How Jonas looked at her wasn't important. She needed to change and help with the horses. "I think you're delusional, Rhonda." She rushed into her bedroom and threw open her chest of drawers, choosing a T-shirt, some undergarments, and a new pair of jeans.

"How could you not notice that?" Rhonda berated her,

leaning against the doorframe. "He did a double take when he saw you."

"Don't confuse shock with captivation, Rhonda. Me standing in my bra, talking with you, was what took him off guard."

"Miss Ava. The man tripped over his own two feet."

"He's in a hurry," Ava reminded her as she finished zipping her pants. "As am I." She rushed past Rhonda, and the persistent woman followed her through the living room.

"Fine. We don't have to solve this now. We'll talk later. Would you like me to help you with the horses?"

"No, we got this. You just get on the horn and make those calls, and I'll help you when I get back. Oh, and can you make another pot of coffee? I have a feeling it's going to be long day."

"Of course. And Miss Ava?"

Ava stopped at the kitchen door and looked at Rhonda, uncertain what the woman could possibly say next. "Yeah?"

"You're a beautiful, hard-working, loyal woman. And any man would consider himself lucky to have you. Don't forget that."

Ava smiled and allowed Rhonda's compliment to register in all the right places. It reminded her of what her father used to tell her so many times when the loneliness got too hard to handle. If anyone knew what it felt like to be a single mom craving companionship, it was Rhonda.

She thanked her with heartfelt gratitude and closed the door behind her, all the while longing to feel the comfort and security of Jonas's arms around her. Though she was a mature woman of middle age, she desperately needed the reassurance of his love. With all that was happening on the McKinley ranch, she wasn't so sure she'd ever get it.

****

Four hours later, after Ava and the girls caught and stalled all the horses, fed and mucked each one, they plopped their tired butts at various places on the front porch. Madeline and Jolee snagged the rocking chairs, while Addison and Hayden found comfort leaning against the porch posts.

"You girls want some sandwiches?" Ava asked as she opened the door and stepped inside. A strong, comforting smell of fresh java welcomed her. "There's coffee too, if you want it."

"All of the above," Jolee sighed, leaning back in her chair. "Please."

The rest of the girls chimed in, and Ava took note of

each one's preference when it came to how they liked their coffee and what to hold on the sandwich. Being women, they all seemed to have different tastes.

"I'll tell you what," Ava said, holding up her palm. "I'll bring it all out, and you can make it how you like it."

"I'll help you," Madeline offered as she pushed out of the rocking chair.

Hayden, the youngest of the group, leapt from her place at the post and stole Madeline's seat before her college roommate could. Sinking into the cushion, she rocked back and smiled. "Much better."

"Don't get too comfortable, Hayden," Madeline warned before following Ava inside.

Madeline toed off her boots at the door and looked around the spacious cabin. "Oh, Miss Ava, this is a lovely home."

Ava smiled as she took off her boots as well. "Thank you, Madeline. Although I can't take all the credit. Jonas is actually a neat freak despite the fact that he's a man. I'm lucky in that respect, I guess. I've seen what some bachelor pads can look like."

Madeline laughed. "I'm assuming we're talking about Cole's house?"

"You got it. That man could sure use a woman's help where tidiness is concerned. If only he could find a suitable mate."

Madeline followed Ava into the kitchen. "You'd think given his good looks that he'd be able to snag a good woman."

Ava thought about Cole and his rugged handsomeness that appealed to so many women. He stood well beyond six foot, with a thick head of sable hair and warm brown eyes—the total package for the tall, dark, and handsome cliché.

"It's not that Cole can't snag one. He's just content with one-nighters and flings. He's a man who doesn't like commitment. Steers clear of it, in fact." Ava opened the fridge and piled her arms full of lunch meat, lettuce, tomatoes, and mayo. Turning toward the counter, she dumped the ingredients next to the coffeepot and pulled out a tray from the cabinet below. After that, she grabbed some coffee mugs and considered Cole's bachelor status a little more. "You know, it's a shame, really."

"What's that, Miss Ava?"

"Cole. He's got so much to offer, but he's not willing to share it. Which is strange considering his parents are still happily married after fifty years or so. It's not like he was brought up to think commitment is a bad thing."

Madeline pondered Ava's assessment as she placed the items on a tray. "Did someone special break his heart once?

'Cause guys can really be turned off by that."

"Not that I know of."

Ava and Madeline exchanged looks and smiled. Ava wondered if Madeline would be a nice match for Cole. The possibility seemed a stretch given their age difference of more than ten years. Then again, the age split wasn't so different from what she and Jonas shared.

As quick as the thought entered her mind, she dismissed it. Matchmaking was not her specialty, and she didn't like the idea of dragging Madeline into Cole's spotty love life should he break her heart in the end. She valued Madeline too much to do that to her. Plus, she couldn't even say for sure if the girl was single. For all she knew, Madeline could have a steady boyfriend. Though she worked side by side with all her employees on a regular basis, Ava had never pried into their private lives.

"Should I take out some water bottles for the girls too?" Madeline asked.

Ava plopped a loaf of bread on top of the tray and snapped her fingers. "Yes, water. I believe we have some in here." Ava peered into the fridge again and pulled out five bottles.

Just as they headed for the door, Rhonda came around the corner of the hall, talking on the phone.

"Yes. Yes, here she is. Hold on one sec, sweetie."

Rhonda offered Ava the phone with an apology. "I'm so sorry, I went ahead and answered your cell. Normally, I would never do that, but it was in the office, and I noticed it was Sawyer. I figured you'd want to take it."

Ava's spirit perked up immediately upon hearing her son's name. "Oh, definitely. Thanks."

Ava juggled the bottles in her left arm as she took the call. "Hey, Sawyer! How are you doing?"

In seeing her struggle, Rhonda gathered the drinks and walked out the door behind Madeline, giving her some privacy.

"I'm great, Mom. A little exhausted with exams, but I can't complain."

Sawyer's voice soothed Ava's heart. She hadn't spoken to him in a while because he'd been cramming for exams, on top of picking up some extra hours at work. Though it had only been a little over a week, she swore his voice changed since she last spoke to him.

"I can't wait to see you. I feel like you've been gone for years." *Forever, actually.* "So, how's school? Hard to believe you only have one more semester. You ready for the big world?"

"Trust me, I'm counting it down. I cannot wait to graduate and be out on my own."

Ava strolled into the living room and made herself

comfortable on the couch. "Have any job prospects lined up yet?"

"Not really. The stable where I work knows I'm looking, but as of right now, they don't have any managerial positions open. I've been getting pretty snug with one of the Thoroughbred owners here. Evidently, his daughter-in-law has an equine therapy practice for disabled children in Lexington. I'm not sure that's what I'm looking for exactly, but it might be a foot in the door."

Hearing her son talk about his plans for a career left her with a feeling of pride. She only wished his father wasn't such an cheapskate for signing over his rights. Despite it being for the best, she still felt Sawyer had always been shortchanged because of it. In his early childhood, he had missed out on so many things that only a father figure could provide a boy. And being a busy traveling mother on the rodeo circuit didn't allow her the freedom to fulfill those needs. She had bills to pay and college to save for, none of which left her much free time for properly rearing a son.

All in all, she could admit Sawyer had turned out just fine without his father in the picture. He was a few months away from graduating college with a bachelor's degree, he had a great head on his shoulders when it came to his finances, and he always managed to make time for her with regular calls. Those things, at least, brought her comfort.

"I'm sure something will pop up for you," Ava said. "Life always has a way of working out."

"To be honest, I'd rather find something closer to home, but I'll take what I can get right now."

Ava sat up straighter. "Closer to home?" She recalled their version of home, which consisted mostly of a three-horse trailer with living quarters during peak rodeo season. They'd either stay in local campgrounds near the shows or room up with friends around the country. They never really had a steady address. Aside from that, he'd spent most of his childhood living with her parents. "Where's home for you, Sawyer?"

He laughed. "Where you and Jonas are, Mom. Where else?"

Ava beamed. "Really? You call Wyoming home?"

"Mom," Sawyer said sincerely, "wherever you are, that's home for me."

A moment of silence filled the air as the two of them relished this mother-son bonding moment. Ava held her emotions back, although she longed to reach through the phone and hug her amazing son.

"Speaking of which," Sawyer interjected, "how is Jonas these days? Busier than a puppy with two peckers, I'd imagine."

"Sawyer," Ava scolded.

"Really, Mom. I'm twenty-two years old. I think I'm old enough to say pecker now."

"Not around me, you're not."

She heard her son sigh. "Yes, ma'am."

"That's better. But, yes, Jonas is extremely busy. We have an issue with a grizzly right now, and I'm not sure how we're going to fix it."

"A grizzly? Cool! I'd love to see one of those up close."

Ava enjoyed Sawyer's naiveté about large wild predators as it brought out the young, curious boy in him, but she knew well there was nothing "cool" about it, especially when it was so close to home. "As beautiful as grizzlies are, this one's a little too brave," she explained. "She's a mama with two cubs, and she got a hold of Cole's dog yesterday."

"Oh no. That's not good. Is he all right?"

Ava squished herself back into the cushion of the couch. "Yeah, he's okay. Cole brought him home from the vet's this morning, but he spent the night under Doc Peterson's care. Had to be stitched up."

"Wow, that bad, huh? Do you need me to fly out there? I can lend a hand."

The protective mother in Ava burst forth. "No. You're

not coming out here. You have school to worry about."

"Mom—"

"No," Ava said sternly. "Look, I've got enough to worry about with Jonas and the guys out there with that bear. I don't need to add you to the mix."

"But I can help with the horses and cattle. I'm sure Jonas could use an extra hand taking care of the livestock."

"That's why we have Rod and Brody. I'm serious, Sawyer. We're fine."

Sawyer let out a huff. "Jonas might be fine, but you're not. I can hear it in your voice, Mom. You're stressing about this."

Ava flung her head back on the couch and closed her eyes. She hated that Sawyer could detect her anxiety so easily despite the fact he couldn't even see her. She tried to feign calmness and control. The last thing she wanted was to let her son think she couldn't handle things on the ranch and induce an overwhelming pang of concern for her. He had his studies to worry about, which was more important than the issues she had going on in her life.

"Sawyer, this is Wyoming. Bears come with the territory, and we're working with Fish and Wildlife to try to trap and relocate her to a primary conservation area in Yellowstone. Pretty soon, this will all be over, and it'll be just another day on the ranch."

"Are you sure? 'Cause I have two weeks off from classes right now. It would be real easy for me to fly out there and help you."

"Thank you, son. But we've got it under control. My main concern right now is the riding schedule and the money we're losing because of the bear's presence so close to the trails. I'm not sure how long we'll have to postpone that part of the business, but we'll work through it." She glanced at the clock on the wall. "On that note, I really need to get off here. I've got those calls to make."

"All right, well, you take care and keep me up to date on what's happening."

"I will," Ava said, relieved that he agreed to staying put.

"I love you, Mom."

She smiled at hearing his words and was glad he never felt too old to say it. "I love you too, Sawyer."

Chapter Thirteen

Rhonda opened the kitchen door, laughing as she entered. "You girls kill me." She noticed Ava sitting on the couch, and her eyes lit up. "Oh, good, you're finished. How's Sawyer?"

Ava brought her knees up to her chest and hugged her legs. "He's good."

Rhonda came into the living room and sat beside her. She patted Ava's foot and smiled. "Of course he is. He's a wonderful young man. So polite. He had a great mother to teach him."

Ava regarded the woman carefully. She heard an insinuation behind Rhonda's words but wasn't sure what it was. "Where are you going with this?"

"Nowhere," Rhonda insisted.

"Mmhmm. Right."

"Okay, fine. I've been thinking about this whole 'trying to gain Jonas's attention' thing, and clearly we're going about it the wrong way."

"We are?" Ava crossed her arms, unsure of what the woman had in mind. The only thing she did know was that Rhonda was taking her dilemma way too seriously.

"Yes, we are." Rhonda shifted on the couch and faced her. Lively determination highlighted the woman's face. "This whole time, you've been trying to gain his attention by the use of seduction, which works for most men. But let's face it, Jonas is not your ordinary man. We should be concentrating on his long-term memory. You know...the things from the past that drew him to you in the first place. Like when you first met."

Ava narrowed her eyes in curiosity. "All right. You've hooked me. Go on."

Rhonda's smile gleamed with joy. "We all know Jonas is not a pushover. He knows what he likes. Understandably, he found something in you that he just had to have, hence the reason he pursued you. You're a woman of intellect, beauty, and loyalty."

"Quit buttering me up and get to the point."

Rhonda rolled her eyes and slapped her hands on her knees. "Miss Ava. Isn't it obvious? Jonas fell in love with the perfect woman, and you, my dear, have to make him remember why."

Ava's brows rose high. "Isn't that what we were doing?"

"You're not listening."

"I am listening, but I'm not following you. You're speaking in circles."

Rhonda groaned. "Okay, let's try this. Think back to when you first met Jonas. The very first time he spoke to you. It was at the Cheyenne Frontier Days Rodeo, wasn't it? What did he say or do that led you to believe he wanted to get to know you? On a more personal level."

Ava cracked a smile, recalling the scenario. His candid statement echoed in her ears.

The only thing I want right now is to kiss you again. If you'll let me.

There was no way she was going to share Jonas's words with Rhonda. Instead, she provided something less intimate. "He asked me to have coffee with him. And he was pretty adamant about it even though I kept coming up with excuses not to."

Rhonda's head bobbled from side to side as she furrowed her forehead. "Not exactly what I was going for, but it's a start." She tapped her lips with her finger. "Did he say anything that hinted he was attracted to you?"

"Well, he did mention that it was a shame he wouldn't get to see me in spandex that week because my horse came up lame."

"Ooooo, he said that?"

Ava laughed at Rhonda's reaction. "Yeah, he did."

"Hmm...Jonas is as frank as he is handsome. Lucky you. Some men keep that stuff bottled inside." She gave Ava a sideways look. "I bet he's the kind who likes to talk dirty too, huh?"

Ava felt the heat of embarrassment flame her skin, and she bit her lip. "Could we get back to issue at hand?"

Rhonda patted Ava's arm and laughed. "Sorry. This ol' gal likes to dream. Anyway, so he admitted he liked you in your trick riding costumes, right?"

"Yes."

"Perfect. Do you still have them?"

Ava lowered her chin and gave Rhonda a hard look. "I am not putting them on. We're trying to attract Jonas, not repel him. Besides, I couldn't fit into them now if I wanted to."

"Sure you can. It's spandex."

"No." Ava shook her head. "No. No. No. No. No. No. Not happening."

Rhonda ignored her and rose from the couch, heading for the bedroom. "I bet you still keep them in your closet."

Ava chased her down. "I'm not wearing them, no matter what you say."

"Oh, you will, Miss Ava. Especially when I'm done with them." Rhonda opened the walk-in closet door and began sifting through the clothes, sliding hangers to the left as she went.

"What are you talking about?"

Upon finding one, Rhonda pulled it out and held it up. Her lips pursed. "Not the right color." As she chose another, she shook her head and hung it back up. With each costume she pulled out, she critiqued them in succession. "Too flashy. Too sparkly. Whoa, too gaudy!"

Ava grabbed the hanger from Rhonda and defended herself. "I did not pick these out. Our sponsors did."

"I think your sponsors were color blind, honey."

Ava hung it up and slumped against the wall. "They're all like that. And I don't know what you're expecting to find or what you're going to do to—"

"Here we go!" Rhonda cheered. "Now this is a sexy little one."

Ava took one look at the nostalgic costume, and the memories bombarded her every thought. She remembered Jonas's face the first time he saw her in it. The way he looked her up and down when she dismounted from her horse outside the arena. The things he said to her in the barn that night. Things he said he wanted to do with her in that getup, which she could never repeat. It amazed her that Rhonda picked the outfit that was Jonas's favorite.

"I bet he loved this one?" Rhonda inquired. The

smugness on her face said she already knew the answer.

Ava gazed over the black-and-silver ensemble bedazzled with silver sequins, gems, and rhinestones. The sleek, glitzy outfit had been her favorite too.

Once.

Back in the day, she liked how the glossy ebony material streamlined her stocky body and gave her curves a thinner, more contoured look. Now, the conforming fabric would only accentuate the fact that she'd gain a few pounds around the middle as it stretched to accommodate her. "I'm not wearing that."

"You will, and Jonas will go apeshit."

Ava tried hard not to smile. Rhonda's exuberance was downright entertaining. "Apeshit?"

Rhonda chuckled at her own words. "Yes, apeshit. I'm telling you, this right here is the key to all your problems." She reached out and touched Ava's hand the minute she balked. "Just hear me out. Now, I know you look at me and see just a stall mucker, a horse feeder, and an office employee. But you happen to be in the presence of the Park County Fair blue ribbon champion for the advanced sewing category."

"Come again?"

Rhonda held her chin high. "Ask anyone. I'm the whipstitch bitch of Meeteetse."

"That's one heck of a title. You should be proud," Ava said, pouring on the sarcasm. "But how does that pertain to me?"

"It means that I can transform this trick riding outfit into the sexiest lingerie piece you've ever seen."

Ava could hardly believe her ears. The woman was insatiable. "I don't see Victoria's Secret breaking down your door."

Rhonda waved her hand, dismissing the iconic lingerie retailer. "Just give me a few days and I'll prove—" She stopped midsentence. "Wait. You're not sentimental about this costume, are you? I mean, you don't mind if I cut it up and sew on it, do you?"

"Knock yourself out, but I can't guarantee I'll wear it."

Rhonda pressed her palm against her heart as if making a pledge. "Honey, I guarantee you will."

Ava knew there was no dissuading her friend. "Fine. Do what you will with it. But don't think for one second that Jonas won't laugh his butt off when he sees me in it."

"You know better than to think Jonas would do that. He's a gentleman. He would never laugh at you for anything. He loves you."

"I know he loves me," Ava agreed. But did he love her because she was what he had to have? Or because he made do with what he had?

She looked at Rhonda, and for some reason, her emotions came bubbling out. "What if he doesn't love me like he used to? What if after all this trouble, the only thing I end up doing is making him realize I'm not what he wants?"

"If he didn't want you, do you think he'd just keep you around until someone better came along? Give the man some credit, Miss Ava. He's not an asshole. Granted, he might have his head up his ass, but he's not an asshole. Remember that. In the meantime, you start clearing your calendar. Plan a romantic night, just the two of you for this weekend. Oh, and don't forget to wash your hands."

"Wash my hands?"

"Yes, wash your hands. Because when I'm through altering this, one look at you sprawled in his bed with it on will have Jonas eating out of your palm."

Chapter Fourteen

Jonas hung up from the call with Ava and tucked his cell back in his jeans pocket. "All right, boys. Ava's gonna saddle up and meet us at the gate. She'll be there to close it behind us once we're through."

"Is someone going to check on Sammy for me?"

There wasn't much emotion hanging on Cole's question, but Jonas knew better. He nodded once. "Ava's sending Madeline. Is that all right?"

"As long as she knows where the key is."

"I'm sure Ava will tell her."

Cole pushed his hat tighter on his head. "Then I'm good."

As Cole's horse danced impatiently beside him, Jonas took off his hat and swiped his brow with his sleeve, mentally preparing himself for their next task. Under the hot summer sun, driving cattle this late in the day was going to be a scorcher.

While they hadn't been able to keep tabs on the mama

grizzly and her cubs, they were at least able to get Wyoming Fish and Wildlife to acknowledge she was a nuisance bear and needed to be relocated. With Luke and his group setting up culvert traps baited with fresh roadkill at the attack site, Jonas and the guys concentrated on moving Cole's herd to a safer location on the ranch.

Jonas pulled out his handkerchief and soaked it in the cold water left behind by the melting ice in his saddlebag. He couldn't help but recall how Ava had dunked it in the trough and squeezed the water over her chest. The image of her seductive act tantalized him again. If he hadn't had so many responsibilities nagging at him right now, he'd have already slaked that urge.

Jonas tied the cloth around his neck and divvied out the orders. "Brody, you run point. Rod, you and Cole take flank rider positions. Keep the bunch tight. I'll be the drag for any stragglers."

"You got it, hoss," Rod said as he pulled his handkerchief over his mouth and nose and trotted into position on the far side of the herd. Brody nodded without a word of complaint and galloped up ahead, giving the cattle something to follow.

Before Cole took his position on the drive, he rolled up his lariat and looked at Jonas. For the first time in a few days, Jonas saw Cole crack a smile. "Rod told me about what happened to Ava and the trough. I'm just sorry I wasn't there to see it." He finished rolling up the slack in his lariat, pulled up his own kerchief, and slapped his horse's hind end with the stiff rope.

Jonas watched his friend gallop into place at the other side of the herd, wondering if Cole was finally coming to terms with what had happened to Sammy or if the sudden display of humor was just for show. Cole had promised he'd do things by the book when it came to the bear, but Jonas worried the stress of nursing Sammy back to health might take its toll on Cole's good sense.

He couldn't blame him. Sammy was practically Cole's right-hand man on the ranch. If the dog hadn't been injured, he'd be right here in the thick of the drive, heeling cattle along the way. Even Jonas knew he'd miss the canine's assistance in the months ahead. Without Sammy working alongside them, Jonas's job of rounding up the straggling steers with only his horse would be twice as rigorous.

As the four men headed into the open plain, the cattle slowly started to move. Bawls of protest rang out as the steers in the back picked up their heads and inched forward. Those in the front twitched their ears and swished their tails, reluctant to stop grazing. Forced to move onward by the push from behind, the herd finally began to move as a whole.

Using teamwork and patience, the four skilled ranchers drove the herd across miles of terrain like a well-oiled machine. Cole and Rod rode the sides, careful not to bend the herd and destroy the flow, while Jonas maintained it from behind. The only time they slowed the drive was to allow the steers to drink in the creeks or to cross them.

After a couple of hours of trekking over some of Wyoming's most beautiful terrain, they crossed into the last pasture that headed up a ridge on Jonas's property. He loved this particular place on the ranch as it provided the loveliest view of the valley below with the Absaroka mountain range in the distance.

He knew Brody had spent many nights here cooling his jets from the torment his lady friend, Olivia, had put him through. On several occasions, Jonas had found him sleeping in the bed of his truck under the stars, and he swore one of these nights, he'd do the same. He hated that his home had furnished him with such peace and tranquility, and that he hadn't been able to enjoy it because of how many responsibilities ranch life required to run it. Inwardly, he made a promise to himself to make time for those pleasures in the future.

As he tried to envision plans for rest and relaxation in the upcoming weeks, he looked ahead to the front of the herd. About three hundred yards from the gate where Ava said she'd be waiting, Jonas caught sight of Brody waving his arm. Squinting through the harsh sunlight, Jonas determined that his point rider spotted something up ahead in the trees just past the thick brush that lined the fence. It concerned him that something was in the limbs large enough to move them and that neither Ava nor her horse were anywhere in sight.

"Hold up," Jonas called out, pulling back on his reins. "We've got movement in the trees, boys."

Jonas heard Brody shout over the herd of mooing cattle, but the distance between them made it virtually impossible to hear anything he said.

"Did you get that, Rod? What's he saying?"

"Hell if I know," Rod called back. "I think it's his horse."

Jonas watched as Brody fought with his green-broke horse, Psycho. Each time Brody drove his heels into Psycho's flanks, the horse balked and tossed its head, rearing slightly in objection. The spooked horse to the cattle was like a leaf blower to leaves. They turned and bunched together, fighting to find an escape from the commotion.

Jonas brought his hand up to the brim of his hat to shade more of the glaring sun from his eyes. Seeing the trouble Brody had with his mount, he started to regret giving him that damn horse. There were tons of better steeds on this ranch more suited for driving cattle, but Jonas had been so impressed with Brody's horse-handling skills a few weeks back that he figured the man deserved to own the horse he broke.

He watched Brody rein Psycho in a tight circle multiple times, then urge him forward toward the trees. The limbs shook with vigor, and Psycho snorted and backed up.

"Please tell me we don't have another bear on our hands," Jonas grumbled under his breath. As soon as the words fell from his mouth, he saw Cole draw his rifle from the side of his saddle, obviously fearing the same.

"Cole," Jonas warned.

"Chill out, McKinley. You know I never take a shot unless I know what's at the end of the barrel."

Jonas turned his attention to Rod, who had already retrieved his binoculars from his horn bag. "What do you see, Rod? We got another bear?"

Rod gazed through the binoculars for a few more seconds before answering. "Not unless bears are wearing pretty black bras these days."

"What?"

Rod let out a laugh. "You're not going to believe this, hoss, but I think that's your Ava in the tree."

"Ava?" Jonas's heart jumped to his throat. His attention suddenly flew to Cole, who had his weapon drawn. "Cole! Lower your weapon! It's Ava!"

Cole dropped the barrel of his gun toward the ground. "What the hell's she doing?"

Jonas kicked Winchester's flanks and sped toward Rod. The thought of Ava in Cole's steel sights had him biting down so hard, he thought his teeth would crack under the pressure. But knowing Rod might be checking her out with the use of binoculars boiled his blood even more.

"I can't say for sure," Rod said as Winchester skidded to a halt beside him, "but whatever she's doing, it's without a shirt."

Rod's horse danced beneath him as Jonas sidled Winchester up close, but Rod didn't falter with the binoculars. "You gotta get a look at this, McKinley. She's standing on her horse in nothing but a black bra. What kind of trick riding does she call this?"

Jonas could hardly believe that Ava was in the tree, much less without a shirt. She was as modest as they came, and no amount of convincing could make her do something this crazy.

Jonas wanted to believe Rod was only pulling his leg. He reached over and ripped the binoculars from Rod's hand. "Give me those!"

Jonas gazed through them and tweaked the focus dial. If he hadn't seen it with his own eyes, he never would've believed it. Ava, sure as shooting, stood on her horse's back, topless. At chest level, her shirt blew in the breeze strung from the limb of tree.

"And you thought I was kidding," Rod jeered, slapping his leg.

Jonas threw the binoculars back at Rod. Chaos now ensued. Cattle aimlessly dispersed from the herd and began grazing in small groups. Jonas cussed and reined his horse around Rod. "Help Cole and Brody round these steers up. I'll ride ahead and find out what the hell Ava's doing."

Behind him, Jonas heard Rod laugh over the sound of hoofbeats. He now understood why Brody was often in fits with his older brother. Rod was a standup guy, and one of the hardest working men he knew, but damned if the taunts and jokes didn't get old.

Jonas grunted a signal to his horse, and Winchester broke into a fast gallop toward the top of the ridge. In the sprint there, his mind raced. No amount of figuring could sum up what Ava was doing with her shirt off, knowing he and the guys would be coming through with a herd of steers.

Was she trying to piss him off? Or maybe she was trying to tempt him again like she'd done at the water trough earlier this morning? And if she was, why did she pick this opportunity to do it? The guys were with him, for Christ's sake!

Ava, of all people, knew that when it came to cattle, they spooked easily. He'd made the call to her earlier and told her to lay low a safe distance from the gate so she could close it behind them—like she'd done many times before.

She knew how to do this.

And she knew this wasn't the time to be horsing around.

With all the crazy things Ava had said and done that week, there was no telling what the woman was up to. First, it was that they were too comfortable. Then they weren't close enough. And then, without him really understanding why, she fell into the water trough trying to be seductive. Sure, he enjoyed the little erotic show—the squeezing of water droplets over her chest, the sensual way she leaned back and gave him a clear view of the moisture rolling down between her breasts. He would've enjoyed it a heck of a lot more had Brody and Rod not been there to witness it as well. But no matter how many times he tried to interpret Ava's actions, he always came up short.

Jonas shook the extraneous thoughts from his brain and slowed his horse as he rode through the gate. Along the fence line, thick brush grew up in a tangled mess, concealing the five strands of barbed wire his father had strung more than twenty years ago.

For a quick second, he made a mental note to get out there soon and spray his fencerows before it got out of control.

That thought quickly dispersed when Ava's horse shook, and she called out in frustration, "Ranger, dammit. Stop it!"

Jonas urged Winchester forward, knowing Ava had no idea he rode up. A beautiful plain of creamy skin, divided only by the black strap of her bra across her back, came into his view. Through the leafy tree limbs, he could see her struggling to stand on her horse's back while tugging on her shirt that was hung up in the limb beside her. Though it was definitely within reach, Jonas imagined Ranger was taking cues from her position on his back. He'd been trained all his life to run the minute she stood.

All anger drained from his body. He wanted to laugh at her dilemma but thought she'd only get mad. Hiding his amusement, he softly cleared his throat.

Ava whipped her head around and gasped, nearly toppling from her horse's back. She grasped the flimsy limb for balance as Ranger stepped forward, only to teeter and squall in fright. But, just like in her trick riding days, she quickly recovered. Squatting low on the saddle with her feet braced on either side, she covered her breasts with her arms.

"This is *not* what it looks like, Jonas."

Chapter Fifteen

Jonas couldn't tell if Ava was mad or embarrassed.
Maybe a little of both.

He pulled down the handkerchief around his face and smiled. "It looks like you're losing a fight with a tree. But I can't figure out how in the world this scuffle started in the first place. All you were supposed to do was lay low until the cattle came through." He glanced upward into the tree. "And yet, you manage to rip your shirt clean off and halt the drive."

Ava heaved a heavy sigh. "I was waiting for you guys to come, staying out of sight in the brush, and my shirt got caught. I couldn't free it no matter what I did, so I slipped my arms out of the sleeves. I tried to untangle it, but Ranger here wouldn't stand still long enough for me to do that."

"He's only doing what he's been taught."

Ava scowled at him. "Don't you think I know that, Jonas?"

"Well, do you know that Cole drew his rifle fearing you were a bear?"

Ava's eyes widened. "Are you kidding me?"

"I wish I was, Trick. This could've turned ugly mighty fast. Lucky for you, Cole's not trigger happy."

She hung her head in her hands. "Look, you can browbeat me all you want because I know I completely messed up here, but can you just hold it until later? I really would like to get my shirt before the guys see me."

"It's too late for that," Jonas said as he dismounted. "Rod got a nice long look at you with his binoculars before I could stop him."

As he walked up to Ranger and petted his muzzle, Jonas noticed the vein in Ava's temple. It was a dead giveaway that she'd been fighting with her shirt for long enough and didn't need any more grief. Knowing he wasn't the only one who enjoyed her little peep show was punishment enough.

He reached for her waist and helped her dismount. Her warm bare skin felt soft and smooth beneath his callused hands. He wished he could caress more of her than just the curvy sides of her torso, but he didn't trust that Rod had put away his binoculars. He stroked the back of his hand across her cheek instead.

"You know...I have half a mind to take you right

here." He couldn't help but look at the plump mounds of her breasts tucked inside the cups of her black demi bra. The contrast of the dark fabric against her fair, freckled skin wreaked havoc on him. Though he'd seen her many times this way, it had been years since he'd seen her this way out in the open.

Her auburn hair shone like fire under the summer sun, and her supple skin glistened with perspiration. What he wouldn't give to pull out the elastic band securing her long locks and let them cascade around her shoulders. He loved the idea of fisting her soft tresses in his hands and backing her against the tree.

"If you have a mind to take me, why don't you, McKinley?"

Ava's voice was as delicate as a feather but as potent as a fist to the gut. He wondered where this side of her had come from, and he wasn't sure he liked it. Point blank, the shock of her bald-faced nerve made him hesitate more than react. As much as he'd like to assume she had primal urges that needed satisfying, this wasn't the time or place to be knocking boots.

He took a step back and grabbed Ranger's reins. "I can't. We can't. You know this."

The look on her face pinched his heart. He saw utter disappointment in her eyes and perhaps a trace of sadness, as if he'd flat-out rejected her. Immediately, he amended his words.

"It's not that I don't want to. Believe me. I'm *dying* to. But the guys—the cattle—it's just…"

Ava's chin dropped, and she sighed. "I know. It's always this way."

He cradled her face in his palms and lifted it. "It doesn't have to be. Let's plan a quiet night, just the two of us. We can even come back out here if we want."

Jonas was glad to see he'd pulled a smile from her. "Really?"

"Sure, why not?" As soon as the words came out of his mouth, he remembered the threat of the grizzly. "Actually, scratch that. We have a bear in our midst. But the day we catch and relocate her, we'll celebrate right here. On this ridge. We'll lay a blanket down under this very tree. We might have to pitchfork a few cow patties out of the way, but let's do it, Trick. Is it a date?"

Ava's smile beamed. "I'd like that very much, Jonas."

"Good. Now hold your horse so I can get your shirt down."

Ava moved out of his way and held Ranger by his bridle to steady him. As Jonas mounted, she watched him move with athletic grace on top of a twelve-hundred-pound animal, balancing on the seat of her saddle as he stood to reach the snarled garment.

Ranger tried to lower his head and move forward, but she halted him. "Easy, boy."

She held firm to his bridle as Jonas untangled the fabric, getting a good look at his perfect body in the meantime. His blue plaid shirt, rolled up at the elbows, did little to hide the broad shoulders and long, muscular arms beneath. His weathered chaps helped to accentuate his taut, round butt while his tight Levis molded to it in the most alluring way. Little did Jonas know his western apparel tempted her more than if he were dressed in a tuxedo. Most women melted for a sharp-dressed man, but she swooned for her cowboy in dusty leather and denim.

Images of lying beneath Jonas on a blanket under this very tree filled her mind. She couldn't wait to spend an evening with him on this ridge. She only hoped it would be soon.

"Um, Trick...I think you've got a problem."

Ava blinked away her thoughts. "Oh yeah? What's that?"

Jonas held up her tattered shirt with both hands. The gentle breeze blew the fabric just enough to reveal a sizeable rip in the back and one sleeve hanging by a thread.

"There's not a single button left on it."

His dimples popped as he smiled, and his eyes glittered like sapphires. He never looked sexier than he did right then.

"There's no way that will cover these girls." Ava gestured. "Any chance you can ride back to the house and get me a different one?"

Jonas squatted on his haunches, grabbed the horn, and hopped down. "Not a chance. Here, take mine."

The second he popped the first button of his shirt, Ava's mouth watered. Her gaze fell on the ripples of muscles in his stomach showing as he unfastened each one.

She stood motionless as he ambled close and wrapped his shirt around her shoulders. She could practically feel the heat from his body radiating over hers as he stood in front of her. Feeding her arms through the sleeves, she was unable to peel her eyes from his gorgeous physique. No denying, Jonas had the body of a swimmer, the definition of a gymnast, and the cocky self-assurance of a bull rider.

"Quit thinking of screwing me, Trick," he said with the brashest of grins.

And the mouth of a sailor, Ava added to herself. "You don't know if that's really what I'm thinking."

He dipped his head and whispered in her ear, "Sure I do. I can see it in your eyes."

Ava struggled to keep a straight face. He claimed he knew her well enough to know what she was thinking, but did he know how badly she missed him? Or that she wished he'd stop working for just a few hours and spend a little time with her? Did he know she needed a long night of love making more than just the fantasy of it? He'd lit her afire and put her on the back burner for too long, and it was high time to make things happen.

Ava seized him by his belt loops and pulled him close. If there was one thing she knew about Jonas, it was that he always had to have the upper hand. Always had to have control. His statement about her naughty thoughts might have been purely presumptuous on his part and even a little egotistical, but her response would soon put her back in the driver's seat.

She tipped her mouth just under his earlobe and whispered against his neck, "What if I can't stop thinking about screwing you? What will you do then?"

Jonas straightened and groaned. She saw the muscles in his jaw clench. He grabbed her by the arms and held her firm against his chest. She felt the rise and fall of his deep breaths and noticed the way he zeroed in on her lips. He waged an inner duel between the work he had to finish and the pleasures he wanted to take for himself. It almost looked as if the team led by his hormones was about to win, but he released his grip and stepped backward.

"You're killing me, Trick," he said, stomping past his horse and toward the gate with a precarious hitch in his step.

She laughed while quickly buttoning Jonas's shirt. At least she'd finally made some headway in getting him to notice her. Sparking his interest and keeping him from boredom was something she'd wanted all along.

Jonas looked back at her before he stopped at the clearing in the fence line, having enough sense to make sure she was fully clothed before waving the guys through. He stood there with his hands on his hips, his bare chest exposed for all to see.

Within a few seconds, Brody trotted through with the herd of Black Angus steers behind him. As Cole and Rod brought up the rear, they whistled and cat-called at Jonas for fun.

"Lookin' good, hoss," Rod said.

Jonas flipped Rod the bird as he swung the gate closed. Rod caught sight of Ava standing beside her horse beneath the tree and tipped his hat as he trotted by.

Ava waved but paid no mind to Rod's antics. Her shirtless cowboy held more of her attention as he traipsed through the grassy field toward her. His long arms swung with each step, and his chaps flapped at his calves, making him look like a man on a mission.

Once he approached, she handed him the reins to his horse, and they both mounted their respective steeds. She tucked her torn shirt in her horn bag and met his gaze with a smile. "Thanks for the shirt."

Jonas adjusted his Stetson and grinned. "All in a day's work."

He clicked his tongue twice, and Winchester trotted forward, eventually into a canter, to catch up with the other horses. Ava admired the man loping across the ridge, her thoughts lost in the rhythmic movement of his agile body as the sunlight kissed the smooth, bare skin of his back and shoulders.

She sighed with total contentment, pleased that she'd finally attained a better outlook on their relationship. She hoped to breathe new life into it using a little bit of imagination, a lot of guts, and the trick riding outfit Rhonda had suggested. She could only pray it wouldn't blow up in her face like the other attempts she'd made.

Chapter Sixteen

For the duration of the week, Ava kept to herself and put her nose to the grindstone. It was better this way. Work kept her mind occupied and less likely to drift onto paths that led toward distraction. Distractions were bad on a working ranch, especially when there were already hundreds of them, with big brown eyes, needing constant care in the pastures and barns.

Despite the urge to panic about her upcoming surprise for Jonas involving her trick riding outfit, Rhonda had assured her the alterations were going smoothly and that she'd be finished by Saturday. Ava's only job was to be ready.

Ava was certainly ready, but she was also nervous. She had never done anything like this before, and the thought of looking a fool in front of Jonas had her on the verge of freaking out. Given her track record thus far, she wasn't sure she possessed the confidence this kind of night required.

To maintain sanity, Ava took care of the numerous small jobs on the ranch that were often put off. Over time, they had multiplied, and she was determined to keep anything from getting in the way of her special surprise weekend. She tightened wobbly gate hinges, swept out dusty old cobwebs in the rafters and stalls, bathed muddy horses, and checked their hoof lengths. Noticing that a large portion of them needed resetting, she also called the farrier.

In the meantime, Rhonda caught up with two weeks' worth of cancellation calls and organized Ava's office. Madeline and Jolee cleaned and oiled saddles, while Addison and Hayden singlehandedly took on the feeding and mucking.

By Friday afternoon, half the horse herd had been shod, all the gear and harnesses in the tack room had been cleaned, the barn tidied up, and all minor maintenance related to the many buildings had been completed.

Jonas, unaware of Ava's grand scheme, spent the better part of his week vaccinating cattle with Cole and spraying fencerows with Brody and Rod. Ava hardly saw him during the daylight hours except in passing, and when she did have the opportunity to have a conversation with him, he was a zombie, often nodding off to sleep.

When Saturday morning rolled around, Ava woke up

minutes before the alarm went off, excited and full of jitters. After slipping from the bed, she tiptoed to the kitchen and made a pot of coffee.

Fifteen minutes later, she came back and sat on the bed next to Jonas. He hadn't moved and was lying on his back with the covers at his waist, his head slightly turned to the side. For a few quiet minutes, she watched him sleep, marveling at his restful form and stunning good looks. She regarded the sharp angles of his face, the color of his beautifully tan skin, the dusting of blond hair on his muscular arms and chest.

"How long are you going to sit there and watch me sleep, Trick?"

Ava flinched at the sound of his voice and swatted at him. "As long as I want. I feel like I haven't seen you." She bent and laid her head upon his chest, stealing some of his body's warmth for herself.

She felt the weight of his arm drape across her back. "You see me every night before we close our eyes."

"Yeah, well, it would be nice to see you longer than two minutes, because that's about as much time as I get from you after you hit the pillow."

"I'm sorry, baby. We've just been hitting it hard."

"I don't foresee it getting any better. Once fall hits, we'll be working that much harder to prepare for winter."

"So, what are you saying?"

The sound of his groggy voice vibrated against her ear. She cherished that lazy hum and wished they could stay in bed all day. "I'm saying the work will never cease no matter what time of year it is, so somehow we have to make time for each other."

"Like we're doing right now?"

Jonas rolled his body and pulled Ava with him. He landed on top of her with the bulk of his upper body supported on his elbows. She giggled beneath him, enjoying the heavy weight of his lower half pinning her to the bed.

She stroked the muscles flexing in his biceps. "Yes, like we're doing right now. Isn't this nice?"

"Nice?" He moved his hips against hers. "Nice, isn't what I'd call *this*."

Ava reached around and clutched the tight cheeks of his bottom, pulling him closer. "What *do* you call it, then?"

A truck horn sounded in the driveway. Seconds later, a vehicle door slammed and a dog barked. Jonas sighed with disappointment and rolled off Ava onto his back. "I call it cruel."

Ava squeezed her eyes shut, cursing their timing. "Is that Cole?"

"Sounds like it. Sammy too. He's early." Jonas dragged his hands down his face and garbled a string of curse words before speaking. "Trick, we can make time for each other all we want, but until we either sell all we own or kill all our friends, we'll never have time alone."

Ava laid her hand on Jonas's stomach, soothing him, though she was just as irritated. "You're right. Let's just kill 'em all. I know a good place to bury them."

Together, they laughed at the cynical joke and rolled out of bed on their respective sides. The sound of Sammy's paws hit the front porch, followed by the thump of Cole's boots as he climbed the three stairs and rapped on the door.

Jonas shook his head. "We've got to find that man a woman." Sammy's sharp bark split through the walls of the cabin. "A shy, quiet woman," he added as he stretched.

Ava met him at the foot of the bed and wrapped her arms around his waist. On tiptoes, she kissed his lips. "I'd prefer to find some time with you."

Jonas brushed back her hair and cradled her face in his palms. "What is that? This time thing you keep mentioning. I'm lost to what that is."

She slugged his gut. "I'm serious, Jonas."

He tightened his stomach and laughed it off, pulling her into a warm hug. "I know you are, but I don't know how to do that. I can't just neglect the farm."

"I'm not asking you to," Ava said, looking up at him

with sincerity. "Just take a little time off here and there. A few hours at the end of the day. Nothing big, maybe a couple of times a month. Starting tonight." She spoke sternly, making sure he'd have no room to negotiate, but smiled in a way that hopefully pulled on his heart strings.

"Tonight," Jonas repeated as if he were running its availability status on his mental calendar.

"Yes, tonight. Just you and me. We'll tell everyone to go home early—with the understanding that under no circumstances do they return."

Jonas's laughter lightened her heart, and she actually felt him leaning toward the idea. She drew playful circles around his navel.

"I'll open a bottle of wine...we can grill a couple steaks...and then," she said, sliding her hand down between his legs and giving him a good, hard squeeze, "we can continue our discussion on how *nice* this was, before we were so rudely interrupted."

Cole knocked again, this time a little harder.

Jonas growled and fisted his hands in her hair. He pulled just enough to stretch out her neck and bury his face there, playfully biting up and down the taut tendons running along her throat.

Ava squirmed in his arms, and the more he confined her escape, the more she giggled. She could hardly contain her joy. Having his arms locked around her with the promise of some alone time this evening sent her heart skyrocketing.

After a few moments of playful grappling, Jonas finally released her and lumbered toward the bathroom. Her gaze dropped to his perfectly round butt before he disappeared through the door.

She ran over and peeked inside, getting one last glimpse of his deliciously naked body. "What time should I be ready?"

Jonas snickered at her question, as if a few ideas of what she should be ready for had already formulated in his head. "We have more fencerows to spray today. Since Cole's here early, we should get finished by six."

Cole beat on the door now.

Jonas grabbed a towel from the wall rack and swung it around his waist. "Go answer the door, Trick, before Cole breaks it down. You'll get your fill of this tonight."

"Fine. But I warn you," she said, pointing, "no excuses. No changing plans. Got it?"

"Oh, I got it, all right. I got it *bad*. Now get out so I can figure out how to piss with this."

Chapter Seventeen

Ava snagged her robe from the foot of the bed and made her way through the living room to answer Cole pounding on the door. At his right, attached to a leash, Sammy sat obediently at his feet with his bad leg sticking out to the side. A cumbersome white lampshade guard encircled his neck, but he didn't seem to mind. With his tongue dangling to the side, there seemed to be a contented smile on the dog's face, as if he were happy to be active in the fresh air with his owner.

Ava tightened the robe at her waist and opened the back door. "Hey, Cole. Hey, Sammy. How are you doing, you poor sweet thing?"

Sammy leapt forward to meet her outstretched hand, uninhibited by his injured back leg. She squatted down and rubbed his stout, muscular chest, as the lampshade made it difficult for her to give a good scratching behind the ears. Sammy held his toothy smile and panted, delighting in any attention she wished to give. His tail wagged hard, swinging his hind back and forth through momentum.

Ava regarded the jagged lines of stitches zigzagging around his leg and cringed. "Oh, Cole. That bear got a hold of him good."

Cole squatted beside her and joined the rub fest. "Yeah, but she didn't get the best of him. Ain't that right, Sammy boy?"

Sammy let out a sharp bark in agreement, then two more for good measure.

Cole clenched a playful fist around Sammy's muzzle. "All right, all right. We heard you, boy. That's enough."

As Cole went back to loving on his dog, Ava noticed a glint of joy and relief in his eyes. She pitied the bachelor for the stress he went through the past couple of days, with no one to comfort him. She kicked herself for not being a good friend and visiting. She wondered how long it had been since the man had a good home-cooked meal.

She opened her mouth to offer an invitation for this evening, but closed it right away. Tonight was her night with Jonas. *No excuses. No changing plans.* Cole had already interrupted them once this week—twice if you count this morning. Once was enough.

She turned her attention back to Sammy and his injured leg. "Looks like he's getting around pretty good. If he's in any pain, he sure doesn't show it."

Cole gave the dog a few manly pats and stood. "Doc says he shouldn't need much pain medication now that he's up and around. But he has to stay on a leash until the sutures come out." Cole wiggled the leash and smiled at Sammy. "It's damn near killing him to be tied to my side. He's used to free ranging, you know. But it won't be long. Another week and he'll be free of those stitches. Back to chasing rabbits and running circles around me, won't you, boy?"

Sammy barked an affirmative and received a loving pat on the head from his owner. Ava smiled at the tight bond between Cole and his trusty Blue Heeler. Their fondness for each other was darn near palpable. As she acknowledged the profound relationship between man and dog, she wondered about her own with Jonas.

Could anyone else see and feel the connection she had with him?

Would they even be able to tell that they were a couple?

Could they say to themselves, *Now that is a pair who truly love each other?*

When she and Jonas had first gotten together, she could answer yes to all three. But after seven years of living with him, she wasn't so sure anymore.

Ava came to her feet, and a sudden concern for

Sammy's well-being slipped in. "You're not going to take him with you guys, are you?"

Cole took off his cowboy hat and pressed it to his chest. "Well, I was if you weren't going to be home. But I don't want you to go out of your way. He'll be fine in the back of the Gator if—"

"Nonsense," she said with a downward wave of her hand. "I'd be happy to watch him."

"Are you sure? I don't want to trouble you none."

"It's no trouble at all." Ava bent at the waist and stroked Sammy's head. "As long as he's all right staying with me."

Cole righted his hat back on his head. "Well, you'll have to take him inside so he doesn't see me leave on the Gator. He'll bark all day if he knows I left him."

Ava brought to mind the piercing sound of Sammy's bark and couldn't imagine a whole day of it. "No, we definitely wouldn't want that, would we, boy?" She petted his head again and took the leash from Cole. "I've got some coffee made. Care for a cup?"

Cole shook his head. "I'm good." He peeked around her shoulder inside the house. "What the hell's taking Jonas so long in there?"

Ava hid her smile. "I'm sure he'll be out soon." She cleared her throat and changed the subject. "Did you bring any medication for Sammy?"

"Oh yeah. Right." Cole reached into his pocket and pulled out four assorted pills. Again, Ava tried not to smile. Only a man would think to pocket a bunch of pills instead of just bringing the whole bottle labeled with directions.

Holding out his palm, he pointed to each pair, describing their purpose. "These are his pain meds. He already had his morning dose, but you can give him more later if you think he needs it. Make sure it's with food."

"Got it."

"And these are his antibiotics. He'll need a dose this afternoon and another this evening if I'm not back in time."

Ava recalled Jonas's words. *"You'll get your fill of this tonight."* If Jonas was serious, Cole would definitely be back in time to give Sammy the last dose of antibiotics.

She hoped so, anyway.

Too many times, her hopes had been squashed.

As she scooped the loose pills from Cole's hand, Jonas came up behind her. He put his hands on her shoulders and squeezed himself between her body and the doorframe. "You ready?"

Jonas's deep voice resonated within her as she felt his torso brush against her back. She turned to kiss him good-bye, but he was already descending the porch steps with

Cole on his heels.

"Been ready all morning," Cole said with disdain. "What the hell were you doing in there? Curling your hair?"

"Nothing that concerns you." Jonas glanced back at Ava leading Sammy inside, winked, and waved good-bye.

****

It was no surprise to Ava that Sammy lingered at the kitchen door, waiting for Cole. Though he whined on occasion, like when he heard each of the girls pull up for work later that morning, he never barked. The most he did was shuffle between the window and the door, keeping a keen eye on the familiar truck in the driveway. As long as he saw Cole's black Ford, he knew he hadn't been left behind.

All morning, he kept up the routine of whining, pacing, and pouting. The only time he didn't succumb to the needy behavior was when Ava headed to the barn to feed. There, the girls took turns caring for him, gushing over him, pampering him. He received more attention that afternoon than he ever had in his life.

By late afternoon, the steers had been grained, the horses hayed, and the stalls mucked. Addison and Hayden left right away to meet family for dinner, Jolee left a half hour later to visit her boyfriend, but Madeline lingered around the farm to lie in the grass and soak up a little sunshine with Sammy.

As Ava walked to the house, she wondered when Rhonda would arrive and pulled out her phone. It was getting close to six o'clock and she still hadn't heard from her. She'd never been too keen on the idea of wearing lingerie, but now that Rhonda had put the idea in her head, she could admit to being excited.

At the sound of Sammy's barking, she turned around and saw Rhonda. She pocketed her cell and met her on the drive, anxious to see her friend's handiwork. Ava couldn't stop smiling, though she wasn't exactly sure why.

Rhonda stepped out of her car and handed Ava a gift bag. She glanced at Madeline sitting on the lawn and waved. "You might want to wait until you get inside before you open it," she advised.

"Oh Lord, is it that obscene?"

Rhonda ushered her toward the house. "It's not obscene. But it could be considered skimpy."

Ava panicked. "I can't do skimpy."

"Yes, you can. Think of how happy Jonas will be to see you in skimpy."

Chapter Eighteen

Jonas steered the Gator under the lean-to and killed the engine. He and Cole unhooked the empty tank from the cargo box of the utility vehicle and sprayed the residual chemicals from it, the hose, and the nozzle. With time to spare, he and Cole lowered the tailgate and drank a beer, discussing work plans for the next week.

As they determined priorities—between spraying fencerows and splitting firewood—Jonas reminded him they needed to wrap things up. He had plans tonight with Ava and didn't want to make her wait.

Cole smirked. "You've made her wait for years. What's a few more minutes?"

"What are you talking about?"

"I'm talking about popping the question. A woman like her doesn't want to wait forever."

Jonas shook his head. "Ava? Married? I don't think she wants to be married. She made it perfectly clear when we first got together that she didn't need or want a man to take care of her."

"I didn't say take care of her. I said marry her. There's a difference."

"There is?"

"Sure there is. Marriage is a mutual partnership, give and take. Taking care of someone means that one person in the relationship is dependent on the other. You can be married and still be independent."

Jonas didn't believe Ava saw it that way. "I think she thinks marriage is a burden. That whole ball-and-chain thing."

"Have you asked her what she thinks of it?"

"No."

"Don't you think you should?" Cole took a long swig of his beer. "I thought you wanted to get married?"

"I do. I mean, I did. But I'm good if Ava doesn't want to. It's just a legal document."

"Do what you want, McKinley. But I still think you should talk to Ava about this. You might be surprised what you find out."

Jonas regarded his friend. "No offense, but I'm supposed to take relationship advice from a man who's never had a steady girlfriend?"

"I know, I know. I'd be the first to admit I don't know jack shit about women. But the way Ava's been acting here lately, I think she's wanting something more in the relationship than what she's getting."

"Thanks, Dr. Phil."

The only thing Ava wanted that she wasn't getting was time alone with him. He checked the time display on his cell. Five more minutes.

As he took a swig of his beer, he noticed Madeline and Sammy walking toward them from the front lawn of his house. Cole's dog limped on three legs with his nose to the ground, sniffing, eager to find something to chase.

Jonas laughed at the poor pooch. No matter how much Madeline tried to hold his head up with the leash, he kept scooping gravel into the pet cone. Despite his intelligence level for heeling cattle, he couldn't seem to figure out that with the Elizabethan collar, he shouldn't sniff the ground. Much like his owner, Sammy proved to be stubborn and insistent.

Jonas nudged Cole and spoke out of the corner of his mouth. "She's cute."

"She's young."

"Yeah, but so was that girl you met down at the Wagon Wheel a few months back. She was still in college too, wasn't she?"

Cole hardly batted an eye. "I don't know. We never talked about college. We didn't talk much at all. That's why

I liked her. She didn't pry into my life, and I didn't care enough to pry into hers. It worked."

"So, what happened?"

"Does it matter?"

Jonas watched Cole finish his beer and crush his can. "I guess it doesn't. I just worry—"

"You don't need to," Cole interrupted. "I'm fine."

Before Jonas could say anything more, Cole tossed his empty can in the back of the Gator and strutted forward, meeting Madeline in front of the barn. He watched his friend drop to his knee and pet his dog. Sammy yapped and wagged his tail, happy to see his owner. Madeline stood with her hands on her hips, smiling at a grown man fussing over his stitched-up dog.

Jonas wondered if Cole would ever settle down or if he'd forever be a bachelor. As Cole would say, there were perks to being unattached. But for Jonas, he could think of a lot more for being in a steady relationship. Like knowing you had someone to come home to instead of an empty house all the time. Or having the benefit of getting laid on a whim.

He thought of Ava and how much his life improved the moment she walked into it—not to mention the improvements she made in his sex life. He couldn't claim it was nonexistent back when he was twenty-three, but he could admit it was often gratuitous and impersonal. He was glad the need for emotionally detached copulation ran out the day he laid eyes on Ava in her black-and-silver-sequined trick riding outfit.

To this day, he couldn't explain it. Something clicked inside him, and he had to have her. In every way imaginable. He wanted her, all of her, heart and soul.

Regardless of Ava's independent nature and need for control, she also brought a form of loyalty he'd never known from a woman. Given he'd inherited the family farm at the tender age of nineteen and was, by normal social standards, a wealthy man before he turned twenty-one, he had to be careful of gold diggers. By all rights, Ava could've been that stereotypical single mother looking for a hot, young sugar daddy to take care of her and her son. He recalled how the talk of the town had once referred to her as the *Colorado Cougar* when she first came around. But that wasn't the case then, and it wasn't the case now.

Though he supported her in every fashion available, Ava was never satisfied to sit back and let him provide for her. Of her own accord, she'd introduced the trail riding business to the ranch, which in turn provided more revenue for other businesses in the area. As far as he was concerned, she was a vital part of his long-term success as well as the seasonal draw for Park County. Second only to

Amelia Earhart, Ava Wallace was undoubtedly the best thing that ever happened to Meeteetse. And, arguably, to him.

He glanced at the gravel lot across from his barn and noted three cars.

Three cars too many.

It was high time they left.

Normally, he welcomed company and encouraged his employees to enjoy the ranch the way his father and grandfather before him had intended. But this night wasn't about social construct or proper behavior.

This was about a good old-fashioned, long-overdue, romp in the hay that neither he nor Ava could enjoy until everyone hit the road.

As luck would have it, he saw Rhonda exiting his house from the front porch. He met her at her car and opened the door for her, hoping to speed things along. "Ma'am."

Rhonda smiled and patted his arm. "Well, aren't you just the sweetest." She gave him a sideways look as she climbed in the front seat. "Have fun tonight, Mr. McKinley."

Jonas closed her door, trying to discern if he detected a hint of subliminal suggestion in the woman's words or not. Chances were he read too much into them.

Rhonda rolled her window down and turned the ignition. "Don't keep Miss Ava waiting too long now. You don't want her to get frustrated and ditch this whole thing back in the closet where you'll never see it again."

"Ditch what?"

Rhonda's eyes bulged. "Hell's fire, I've said too much."

Jonas shadowed the car as she backed away. "What are you talking about? What closet?"

Rhonda threw it in Drive and waved nervously. "Forget I said a thing, Mr. McKinley. Bye!"

Cole came up beside him, and they watched her pull away. "What was that all about?"

Jonas removed his Stetson and scratched his head. "I have no idea. Something about the closet and ditching it. Who knows. Ava probably watched some DIY home renovation show on closets and how to say good-bye to the old with a fresh coat of paint and a few well-placed shelves and drawers."

"Sounds expensive," Cole said, slapping his back. "Good luck with that."

"Yeah…thanks."

Cole carefully lifted Sammy onto the front seat of his truck and climbed in behind him. As Cole left for the night, Jonas spun around to check on Madeline's whereabouts. He saw her stretch the hose from inside the barn to top off the horses' water buckets for the night and decided to hurry her along.

"Here, I got that," he said, reaching for the hose.

"Are you sure, Mr. McKinley? I certainly don't mind." She gave one of the horses a pat on its back and smiled. "I love these guys. It's the best job ever."

"I'm glad you think so. I know Ava really likes your dependability and hard work. She's mentioned it to me several times."

"Wow, thanks for telling me."

"You're welcome, Madeline." He watched her back out of the barn, all smiles. "Have a good evening, and see you Monday."

"Yes, sir. Good-bye."

Jonas waved and finished the watering. It took longer than he expected, but he was glad to cross that chore off his list. One less thing to do this evening meant more time with Ava.

Alone time with her.

In bed.

All tangled up in her arms.

As he rolled up the hose and shut off the barn lights, his brain flickered back to Rhonda and the closet she'd mentioned. He really hoped Ava hadn't decided to renovate, and if she had, he doubly hoped she hadn't chosen tonight to start the project. They had more important things to do.

Before he could waste any more brainpower on the issue, he heard the crunch of gravel beneath slow-moving tires. He cussed and marched outside, ready to throw a fit.

Forget a new closet. They needed a gate with a padlock at the entrance of their drive.

Jonas eyed the unfamiliar silver Suburban pulling up beside him. He squinted at the young man in the driver's seat, and until the door opened and he stepped out, Jonas couldn't believe his eyes.

"Sawyer? Is that you?"

Sawyer came to Jonas with outstretched arms. "Behold. It is I, the prodigal son," he joked.

Jonas clasped Sawyer's right hand, shook it hard, and then pulled him into a manly hug. "I'll be damned! Look at you!"

They exchanged a solid beating on the back and laughed in awkward amusement before they separated and gazed at each other in awe.

Jonas wasn't sure what to say. Or feel, for that matter.

Part of him was excited for Ava, as he knew she'd be thrilled to see her son after all this time. But the other part of him couldn't help but envision his own selfish plans going up in smoke. It wasn't like he could tell Sawyer, *Hey.*

Dude. I know you just made a long trip from Lexington, Kentucky but do you think you could come back later so I can shag your mom real quick?

Jonas removed his hat and swiped his brow. "Did your mom know you were coming?"

"Nah, I wanted to surprise her. Is she home?"

Jonas looked up at the house, knowing Ava had been adamant about no excuses, no changes in plans for tonight. He couldn't imagine her sticking to that promise once she knew her son had dropped by.

Of course, he had no idea what she was doing up there. For all he knew, she could be busy cooking a candlelight dinner or even renovating a closet.

Either way, he wasn't gettin' busy tonight.

"Yeah, yeah. She's home."

"Great. Do you mind if I run up there?"

Jonas tried his damnedest to hide his disappointment. "Knock yourself out, kid. Here, I'll grab your luggage. You go see your mom."

Sawyer slapped Jonas on the back. "Thanks, man. You're the best. I can't wait to see the look on mom's face."

Chapter Nineteen

Ava gazed into her dresser mirror at the two-piece lingerie ensemble barely covering her private parts. Rhonda had certainly outdone herself when it came to the alterations. At a glance, it was recognizably a modified version of her favorite trick riding outfit. But after staring at the additional silver-and-black beading, she could barely believe it was once something she wore on the back of a horse.

What amazed her more was looking at her reflection and realizing she looked smokin' hot. Her breasts, supported by a full-figured corset brassiere, plumped up as two perfectly round orbs. The panties were sheer black boy shorts with a thong-style layer of black satin concealing the apex of her thighs. A frilly ruffle of satin edging hung delicately across the round curve of her butt, while sleek garter belts clipped to elegant black hosiery with lacy trim added the perfect visual allure between pretty and provocative.

No doubt about it, Rhonda was a magician with a needle and thread. Ava couldn't wait for Jonas to come in and see her in it.

To complete the look, she slipped her feet into a pair of ebony stilettos from back in her college days. Spinning slowly once more in front of the mirror, she smoothed the feminine ruffles at her hips and pulled each garter, letting them snap against her thighs.

"Rhonda's so right," she purred. "Jonas is gonna go apeshit when he sees this."

Feeling giddy and very anxious for Jonas's reaction, she decided she should dim the lights. Even though she felt unusually confident in her ultra-sexy attire, she was still a flawed forty-year-old woman. No sense in highlighting her imperfections with unflattering bright lighting.

She hoofed it to the kitchen and lit a few candles, setting them in various spots around the house. As she placed the last one on her nightstand next to the bed, she heard the thud of boots climbing the porch steps.

Ava scurried to the light switch next to the bedroom door, turned it off, and leapt onto her bed. She struck a pose, aiming for sensual, but it didn't feel right. Jonas wouldn't want sensual. He'd want the seductress.

With a flip of her hair, she tipped her head and arched her back, bending one of her knees to accentuate the muscle in her calf. Again, it still didn't feel right.

She closed her eyes and tried very hard to envision a position over which Jonas would go nuts. As she attempted to mimic another sexy pose, she heard the front door open and the sound of boots walking through the living room. In a rush to look shameless and exotic, she bent both legs at the knees and crisscrossed her ankles, letting the tips of her heels point toward the ceiling.

She closed her eyes, nearly trembling at the thought of Jonas walking in and seeing her sprawled out on his bed like a Playboy centerfold.

"Hey, Mom! Where are you?"

Ava's eyes shot open. Her body stiffened and her heart thudded to a dead halt.

That sounded like Sawyer! Am I hearing things?

Ava peered around her suspended legs at the same moment Sawyer walked into the bedroom. She screamed, and her son gasped, immediately backpedaling out of the room.

"Oh my gawd, Mom!"

Ava screamed again—because wailing at the top of her lungs seemed like the best response to a very disturbing situation—and hurled herself from the bed. She ran for cover in the bathroom and clutched her racing heart. As she howled in horror, she jogged in place, mortified that her son had seen her this way.

"What's going on in here?" she heard Jonas ask as he stormed into the house. "Ava? Sawyer? You all right?"

"No, I'm not all right!" Sawyer snapped as he paced the other room. "I just walked in on my mom...and she was...well, she was...oh my gawd! My eyes! I saw her all pimped out like an upscale prostitute! Why didn't you tell me she was dressed like that? Better yet, why did you send me up here knowing she was dressed like that?"

"I didn't know she was dressed like that," Jonas insisted. He burst past Sawyer and into the bedroom. "Ava, are you really dressed like a prostitute?" He slid to a halt at the bathroom door, and his brows lifted in surprise when he saw her. "Wow. You *are*." He looked her up and down, and a slow, wicked smile graced his lips. "I mean...I'm glad you are." He swallowed hard. "It certainly doesn't leave much to the imagination, does it? Can you do things in that without taking it off?"

"Seriously, Jonas?" Sawyer barked. "That's my mom you're talking to."

Jonas cringed, but he didn't stop gawking. "My bad."

Ava tried to shield herself, but no matter where she placed her hands, she couldn't hide the copious amounts of flesh her outfit was designed to accentuate. Jonas eyed her like she was a seasoned, grilled steak on Super Bowl

Sunday. He braced his hands on the doorframe and leaned into the bathroom, speaking just above a whisper. "Do you have any idea how hot you look right now? What I want to do to you in that get up?"

"I can still hear you, Jonas!" Sawyer roared. "And it's still just as disturbing! Knock it off!"

Jonas lurched sideways and slammed the bedroom door in Sawyer's face. Ava squeezed her eyes shut, unable to think. Unable to apologize to her son or even look him in the eye. "Oh, this is bad. What do I do? How do I fix this? We have to fix this, Jonas. He'll need therapy. Oh my gosh, he'll need therapy!"

"Calm down," Jonas said, seizing her flailing arms. "He's not going to need therapy. It's not that big a deal."

"For you, maybe," Sawyer argued through the door.

"Oh, Sawyer, I'm so, so sorry," Ava cried, trying to throw her voice enough that her son could hear her. Her words cracked under pressure, and her apology sounded pathetic.

"Trick, listen to me."

"I think I'm gonna be sick. I need air," Sawyer announced and stalked out of the house.

Out of motherly concern, Ava sprang to dart after him, but stopped herself short as soon as she realized she couldn't go anywhere dressed like a hooker. She looked at

Jonas in desperation. "Do something, Jonas."

"Let him go. It's all right," he said, stroking her arms. "He just needs a little space right now."

Ava bit her lip, reliving the scenario over and over in her mind. "I'll never be able to face him."

"Sure you will. In fact, I bet one day, you'll both laugh at this."

Ava shook her head, incapable of believing anything Jonas said to comfort her. She had innocently tried to spice up their relationship with a little visual foreplay, and ended up scarring her son for life.

Her stomach churned. "I'm a horrible mother."

Jonas shook her gently. "Hey. No, you're not. You're an amazing mother. And Sawyer knows that. Right now, it's just a little hard for him to see that, given…" He paused and gestured over her entire body, "all of this is burned into his retinas."

Ava buried her face in Jonas's chest. His attempt at making her laugh only made her feel worse. Deep down, she knew he meant well, but the humiliation of knowing her son had seen her on display in the most inappropriate position ate her alive.

On the verge of having a nervous breakdown, she clung to Jonas. She snuggled into the warmth and familiar scent of his body as her tears fell. He wrapped his strong masculine arms around her, enveloping her in a refuge of quiet consolation. She felt him plant a sweet kiss on the top of her head, and, after a few moments of listening to the steady beat of his heart, the tension in her muscles began to ease.

"Everything is going to be all right," Jonas whispered.

"How do you know?"

"Because I'm going to make sure of it." He lifted her chin and cradled her face. "I'll move mountains to make it happen if I have to. I just don't want you to worry anymore."

She blinked, having a difficult time understanding what exactly Jonas meant to do. "You're going to talk to Sawyer? You'll make sure he's all right?"

"If he'll let me."

"Oh, Jonas," Ava said, relieved. "Thank you." She hugged him as tightly as her weak arms would let her, and he held her close for as long as she needed.

When she eventually pulled away, he reached around the bathroom door and lifted her robe from the hook. He draped it around her shoulders and pulled the fluffy fabric tight beneath her chin.

"I'll be back as soon as I can." He pressed his lips to her forehead and held them there for the span of two breaths before he stepped back.

Ava saw the muscles in his jaw flex and his brows pinch together. He didn't begin to fake how seeing her dressed in skimpy black undergarments and garter belts affected him. The expression on his face moved her. The longing in his eyes shook her to the core.

He didn't want to leave her, that was clear. But he never spoke of it. He simply adjusted his cowboy hat and squared his shoulders. "Don't wait up."

Chapter Twenty

Jonas stepped out onto the front porch and stopped midstride. On the top step, stooping over, Sawyer sat with his head in his hands. Jonas had expected the young man to be as far away from the house as possible, trying to clear his head of thoughts no son wants to have about his mother. It caught him off guard to see him in plain sight.

Jonas planted his hands on his hips and glanced upward. He noticed the first few stars twinkling in the sky as he looked for answers. He knew all there was to know about driving a tractor, plowing a field, firing a rifle, guessing a steer's weight within five pounds, and singing the National Anthem. But he knew nothing about parenting.

When he thought about how he was closer to Sawyer's age than Ava's, the act of nurturing and offering advice seemed completely absurd. Should he speak to Sawyer like a father? Like a friend? Both felt awkward when he tested opening lines in his head.

"If you're standing there trying to figure out what to say to me, Jonas, how 'bout you save it."

Jonas opened his mouth to speak but shut it. A heavy, awkward silence filled the air. As he stood there like an idiot, it became obvious that neither of them wanted to talk about what had happened. There were just some things in life that didn't need rehashing.

Jonas slapped his hands together. "I couldn't agree with you more. So, how about you and I get ourselves a few cold ones down at the Wagon Wheel."

Sawyer looked up as Jonas descended the stairs beside him. "Are you serious?"

"You got a better idea for erasing that picture from your mind?"

Sawyer scoffed. "No."

"Then let's go."

Sawyer stood to follow but hesitated, glancing back at the door. Jonas noted how conflicted the boy was about leaving his mother behind after he'd just arrived.

"Sawyer, she's not going to be mad if you leave. Believe me, she's fighting her own set of demons, being your mother and all. The best thing the both of you can do for each other is walk away for the night. Blow off some steam. Get your drink on."

Sawyer cracked a smile. "Get your drink on?"

"Yeah, isn't that what you college kids say nowadays?"

Sawyer shook his head and laughed. "No one should say that, Jonas. But yeah. I could use a drink."

The two of them walked down to where Jonas's truck was parked and climbed inside. On the drive to the bar, Jonas made several jokes about the vernacular of today's youth, which pulled a few more laughs from Sawyer. It wasn't a topic that necessarily interested Jonas, or held much importance in the grand scheme of things, but it did alleviate the subtle tension that had been forced upon them.

Jonas pulled up to the front of the bar, noting the familiar vehicles in the parking lot. Before he even walked inside, he knew a good portion of the people who were there. Relief washed over him that Cole and Brody were among them. If anything could be avoided by having the guys around, it would be that godawful, awkward silence.

Jonas killed the engine and opened his door, anxious to down that first beer. He'd had one earlier with Cole that evening, but it seemed like forever ago. Before his boots touched the pavement, he heard the time-honored tradition of country music playing on the jukebox and the hard crack of billiard balls on the slate pool table. Neither could drown out the noise of a good time. The place was already alive with drinking, dancing, and, if all went well, a handful of rowdy cowboys looking to have a hog-killin' time.

Jonas walked in first, and the place erupted. Shouts rang out from those who were both happy and surprised to see him. Because of the commotion, Cole looked up from the bank shot he was about to take and lifted his chin in a hello. Then, like it was nothing, he continued with his shot and smoothly pocketed the eight ball for the win.

"Nice shot," Sawyer said from behind Jonas.

Jonas put his arm around Sawyer and led him inside. Bellied up to the bar, he gave Sawyer a few words of advice. "For starters, never play for money against Cole in pool, no matter how much he staggers. You'll lose. Every time."

"Got it."

"And you remember Brody over there, don't ya?" Jonas asked, pointing at the table next to the stage that already had two empty beer bottles on it.

"Oh yeah, the tattooed cowboy."

"Right—but don't call him that. And don't try to drink him under the table either. Few have, and it takes conditioning. We don't have that kind of time tonight."

"Anything else I should know?"

Jonas rubbed his jaw and thought. "Oh yeah. One more thing. If you have to piss? Save water. Go out back."

"Really?"

"Yeah, really."

A cute little bartender with perfect teeth and thick

blonde curls, one whom Jonas had never seen before, walked up to them and smiled. He assumed she was Olivia Langston's replacement after she left for Nashville. He wondered how that waitress change was affecting Brody.

"What'll it be, boys?"

Sawyer sat up straighter on his barstool. "I'd like a Guinness and your phone number, if it's not too much trouble."

Jonas's brows lifted. Around here, no one drank that stout of beer, nor did the women take too kindly to cheesy pickup lines. He was almost embarrassed for the guy. To his surprise, she turned a shade of pink and pulled out a pad of paper from her apron. As she doodled, she spoke in a voice reminiscent of Marilyn Monroe's.

"I'm afraid I can only fill half your order, darlin'," she said, tearing a page and sliding it facedown on the bar. "But maybe your friend here can suggest another brand."

Sawyer never took his eyes off the blonde. "Jonas? What are we drinking tonight?"

Jonas looked at them both and saw sparks flying. He hiked his boot up on the rung of the stool, amazed that he'd suddenly become invisible in a matter of a few seconds. "We'll take a bucket of Bud Lights and four shots of Jack."

"Should I keep a tab open?" she purred, directing her

question to Sawyer.

"That would be great. And if you wouldn't mind, can you bring the drinks out to that table?" Jonas pointed in Brody's direction, and the girl finally tore her gaze from Sawyer.

"I'd be happy to."

As Jonas pulled Sawyer away from the bar, Sawyer flipped over the piece of paper she'd given him. Jonas sneaked a peek for himself and couldn't believe it. She not only provided her number, but her name and the time she'd be getting off as well. "You dog."

"What." Sawyer said. "You're telling me if you were single, you wouldn't have asked for her number?"

"Oh, I'm pretty sure I would've tried to get a number from her, but I think I would've paced myself first. You came out of the gate with it."

"Hey, it worked."

"That it did." Jonas patted Sawyer on the back, astonished by the young stallion's competence for charming a woman's contact information from her with only an opening line. He was also impressed by the blonde's ability to make Sawyer forget the reason they had come here in the first place. He reckoned he'd have to tip her big for that.

As they joined Brody at his table, Jonas reintroduced Ava's son before sitting down. Brody extended his hand,

and Sawyer shook it heartily.

"I haven't seen you in years, Sawyer. It's hard to believe you're all grown up. So, what brings you to Meeteetse?"

He and Jonas exchanged looks. An unspoken agreement that neither would talk about what happened tonight passed between them. Both loved Ava too much to hurt her. Sawyer kicked back in his chair. "Just a guy's night out."

Jonas caught the look Cole sent him from across the pool table as he chalked his cue. No one else saw it, but Jonas knew what it meant. Cole was confused. He was confused about Sawyer's surprise visit, the guy's-night-out excuse, and the fact that Ava wasn't with them, especially when she hadn't seen her son in months.

Jonas also knew Cole wouldn't pry. He was a man of integrity and would never stick his nose where it didn't belong.

"Here you go, gentlemen. A bucket of Bud Lights and four shots of the good stuff," the blonde announced as she set her tray on the table in front of them.

Sawyer was the first to thank her, placing his hand on the small of her back as she emptied the round of drinks. She didn't linger as long as she had at the bar, and that was just as well—for Jonas, anyway. The more he saw Sawyer charming her, engaging her with little touches of his hand, and smelling her sweet perfume amid the staleness of the bar, the more he missed Ava.

He stared at the caramel-colored liquid in his shot glass, the noise around him becoming a constant hum. Alone with his thoughts, he could picture Ava in his button-down shirt, beckoning him to follow her into his bedroom...

He liked that the sleeves were long and the shirttails short, revealing just enough of her butt to attract his gaze to the feminine parts he couldn't see.

Her auburn hair sat piled on the top of her head in a messy bun. Wispy strands framed her beautiful face dotted with faded freckles across her nose. Though she hated them, he cherished every single one, especially those that marked her body, and committed them all to memory.

He itched to kiss her now, but she was giggling. Staying just out of his reach. Playing hard to get, driving him mad.

With one quick lunge forward, he caught her wrist and tugged her into his arms. The soft swell of her curves pressed against his chest as he splayed his hands down her back and over her bottom.

"Dude, Jonas. You in there?"

"Wh—what?" Jonas blinked and realized he had three

guys staring at him, holding their shot glasses in the air.

"Come on, man," Sawyer urged. "You bought them. What are we drinking to?"

Jonas realized that everything he'd just imagined was all in his head. He sat up straighter and raised his glass with his friends, racking his brain for a worthwhile toast on the fly. "To friends…and family."

"And blondes!" Sawyer added.

"Amen to that," Cole concurred.

All four men clinked their glasses together, emptied them in one swift gulp, and slammed them down on the table. Jonas felt the burn slide deep in his chest, and he chased it with a swig of beer. He forced a smile in front of the guys, making it seem as though he were having a great time, when all he was having was withdrawals.

It was going to be a long night without Ava.

Chapter Twenty-one

Sawyer staggered out the door of the bar, and Jonas steadied him. "Easy there, partner."

"I'm fine."

Jonas didn't argue with him, though he knew the man was buzzed. He and Cole chased the shot with only one beer. Brody knocked back a few more by the end of the night, but that was usual for him. Sawyer, on the other hand, drank like it was going out of style. Jonas tried hard to keep an eye on the amount of alcohol he was consuming throughout the evening, but between the crowd of locals coming in and out of the joint, and the four intense games of pool with Cole, he'd lost count.

Pushing the button on his keyless remote, Jonas unlocked the truck and opened the door for Sawyer, watching him climb in the cab like he was climbing into a ball turret from World War II. Jonas tried hard not to laugh at Sawyer's clumsy movements, as he'd been there before. On nights like this, he'd also been on his knees in front of a toilet. He hoped it didn't come to that.

After Sawyer finally situated himself in the seat and ineptly buckled his belt, he gave Jonas the thumbs-up and pulled the truck door shut. Jonas walked around the front and waved good-bye to Cole and Brody, who sat in their trucks, waiting to make sure their assistance wasn't needed before they pulled away.

Jonas followed them out, and for the first few miles, he and Sawyer rode home in silence.

"Jonas?" Sawyer finally prompted.

"Yeah?"

"I want to thank you."

Jonas looked to his right and saw that Sawyer had a serious look on his face. "You don't have to thank me. Thank that cute little waitress back there. She's the one who put that smile on your face. You still got her number, right?"

Sawyer patted his breast pocket. "But that's not what I'm talking about. I want to thank you for taking care of my mom. For giving her a reason to be happy again."

Jonas zeroed in on the last part of Sawyer's words. "There was a time when she wasn't?"

Sawyer's head bobbed with the bumps along the road. His eyelids drooped as he spoke. "Yeah. Back when I was a little boy. She never dated much. There wasn't much time between raising me and traveling the rodeo circuit. But this one guy came along...I don't know, I think I was about thirteen years old. Just a few years before you started dating her..."

Jonas stared at the road ahead, unsure where Sawyer was going with his story about Ava. By the sound of it, he figured it was only going to tick him off. Like any man, he didn't like to know about a woman's past or think of the dude who came before him. What's more, he didn't like knowing someone broke Ava's heart and stole her happiness.

A protective surge of anger balled up in his chest, and his knuckles turned white from gripping the steering wheel so hard. He forced himself to breathe slow and easy, trying not to work himself up. It was ridiculous to do so given this was the past. It wasn't like he could do anything about it now anyway.

"It doesn't matter how old I was," Sawyer continued. "All I know is I was old enough to remember I wanted to kick his ass."

Jonas smiled on the inside. "I can relate to that."

"So anyway, my mom met this guy, some professor or something like that when she was looking into whether or not she should homeschool me, yada yada. You get the drift, and he came off as a real gentleman, you know?

Someone who knew how to treat a woman, old-school kinda deal. Heck, I even fell for him. He tossed ball with me, he took me to all kinds of baseball games, football games. Things a boy needs to do in his life."

Jonas felt a pang of pity for Sawyer. Though he'd lost his own parents in his twenties, he could at least say he'd been with them during the crucial years of his life. "So what happened?"

"My mom came home one night after a date with him. She looked so happy. She had color in her face. That warm glow of contentment. And I remember her coming into my room and talking to me about what I thought of him and if I'd mind if he stayed in our lives on a permanent basis. Being a kid who never knew his father, I was actually thrilled to have a man around who seemed to genuinely care for me, and for my mother."

Jonas waited for the other shoe to drop, never tearing his gaze from the long stretch of winding backroad.

"I don't know what happened exactly, as my mom never said anything, but one minute she was talking about how comfortable she felt with him, the possibility of marriage in her future. Oh, he was comfortable all right. Comfortable with cheating on her."

Jonas went rigid. That damned word came out of Sawyer's mouth just like it had Ava's—reeking with contempt.

Comfortable.

It was no wonder she hated that word. She'd grown to trust this guy with her heart, and then the bastard crushed it.

Comfortable.

It all made sense now. Ava wanted to be closer to him without getting too comfortable, because for her, comfortable was not a positive. It meant that a relationship was on the outs.

He thought about the way she came out to the barn in a push-up bra, trying to grab his attention. Then how she fell into the water trough, trying to be seductive and sexy. And then, if that hadn't done it, she went as far as altering his favorite trick riding outfit into a racy little number with garter belts and heels.

How could he not see the tremendous effort she'd made to be sensuous and provocative, to be what every man fantasized about? He should have noticed way before now.

Cole was right. Ava wanted more. And in thinking they were getting too comfortable in the relationship, she feared she was going to lose him just like she'd lost the professor.

Marriage.

He never gave it a thought because he assumed Ava

was against it. Now, it seemed a possibility.

Jonas thought about making that leap and could actually see himself legally bound to her. The concept of living with one woman for the rest of his life didn't feel suffocating to him. Or dreadful. In fact, it brought a peculiar smile to his face.

"What so funny, Jonas? I just shared something personal with you about my mother and the fact that her heart was ripped to shreds—and you're smiling?"

"No, no... You misunderstand," Jonas said desperately, but Sawyer glared at him.

Jonas panicked and tromped on the brake, pulling over to the side of the road. By the time Jonas whipped it into Park, Sawyer was pushing himself off the dash and trying to open his door.

Jonas grabbed him by the shoulder and yanked him back. "It's not what you think, Sawyer. I wasn't smiling because I found humor in your story. I was smiling because—"

Jonas stopped mid-sentence. It wasn't because he couldn't say the words, but because this was not the way he wanted Sawyer to find out how he really felt.

"Why, Jonas? Why were you smiling?" Sawyer's nostrils flared, and his bloodshot eyes narrowed.

If Sawyer was that protective of his mother, then Jonas

knew he couldn't ask Ava to marry him until he had the boy's approval. Normally, he'd look to Ava's father for a blessing of this magnitude, but since he was deceased, it only made sense to ask Sawyer.

He swallowed hard, uncertain how to initiate the conversation. It scared him to think he might have lost his chance, all because of an untimely smile. He needed Sawyer's support. Without it, he couldn't in good conscience ask Ava.

"Sawyer. When we first got in the truck, you had thanked me for taking care of your mother. For bringing happiness into her life again. Do you remember that?"

Sawyer crossed his arms. "Yeah. I do. Now, I regret ever saying anything."

Jonas's confidence wavered. "I truly hope you don't. I love your mother more than anything in this world—and I wasn't smiling because I was happy. Well, I was happy, but not for the reason you think."

Sawyer stared emotionlessly now. Crediting his detached response as a defense mechanism for the major disappointment and betrayal he had been victim to as a child, Jonas knew he'd better start explaining fast.

"When you told me the story about the professor and your mother, you mentioned her feeling comfortable. And all this week, your mother's been trying to talk to me about our relationship and how she thinks we're *too comfortable* with each other. Being the typical man, I had no idea what she was talking about, and with all the crap that's been going on at the ranch and with the bear, we haven't been able to find the time to really talk it out.

"In the meantime, it seems your mother has tried to fix the situation herself with ways that you've unfortunately walked into."

Sawyer grimaced but didn't interrupt.

"So, by trying to spice things up, I guess she thinks I'll consider her more appealing, which then helps her to think we're not moving into that dreaded *comfortable* stage. Now that I know this about your mother, it has helped me to understand where she's coming from. I have you to thank for that."

He saw Sawyer's posture soften.

"You know your mother better than anyone, I'd imagine. You know she's a very independent woman and doesn't like to rely on others when it comes to her job, her life…her responsibilities to you. She's never given me the impression that she wants more out of our arrangement than what it is currently. That being said, I assumed marriage wasn't something she'd ever want, therefore, I never brought it up. We never discussed it."

"That still doesn't explain why you smiled, Jonas."

"My smile came in thinking perhaps she might be interested in marriage. To me."

Sawyer sat back against the door, his eyes full of questions. "Wait. Are you saying you *want* to marry my mother?"

Jonas thought long and hard. This wasn't a question of bareback or saddle. Bacon or sausage. This was a serious game changer.

His heart warmed to the idea of making Ava a legal partner of the McKinley Ranch. Because the ranch was already a lucrative cattle business passed down from his father, he didn't need her to work. But she did anyway, bringing more income to his table with the horseback riding operation. She was an ambitious woman who deserved to reap the fruits of her labor. Through marriage, she could have all that and more. Whatever he possessed, he wanted her to have the same.

All money aside, he loved Ava and wanted to spend forever with her. There was no one else who could make him feel as happy as she did. As hard as it was for him to fathom, he knew he'd fallen in love with the perfect woman, the only woman he felt—should he dare say—comfortable enough with to share eternity.

Jonas braced his elbow on the back of the truck seat and leaned forward, holding Sawyer's gaze. "Yes. That's exactly what I'm saying. I want to marry your mother. I love her. She makes me happy, and I want to spend the rest of my life making her happy. Now, I totally understand if you'd like to wait until you're sober enough to think about this, but I'm asking you for your mother's hand. Do I have your blessing?"

Chapter Twenty-two

Sawyer started snoring the minute his head hit the pillow. Jonas closed the spare bedroom door as quietly as he could so as not to wake Ava. He found her on the couch, curled up beneath a blanket, with smudges of black mascara on her face.

She'd been crying, and it killed him to know he wasn't here to dry her tears.

He picked her up in his arms and carried her to the bedroom. On the floor lay the sequined bra, the barely there panties, a garter belt, and a pair of heels. Careful not to step on them, he walked to his side of the bed and laid her down.

As he studied the redheaded beauty in funky-colored pajamas, an overwhelming sense of wonder washed over him. He couldn't believe he'd been so lucky to find her. What's more, he couldn't believe she'd stayed. For seven years, he shared his home with her, slept with her, and awoke to the sight of her every morning. That was the extent of their relationship. It was time he gave her more than just camaraderie.

Anxious to be close to her, he undressed and slid in behind her, pulling the covers up over them. She stirred briefly, mewing in her sleep, but never awakened. As he spooned with her, he snuggled against the warmth and softness of her body, planting feathery kisses on her neck.

Without a doubt, he loved this woman.

Closing his eyes to sleep, he thought about how he'd make this day up to her. How he'd prove to her that being comfortable with each other wasn't because of a loss of interest but a natural stage of progression in every healthy, committed relationship.

****

The smell of fresh-brewed coffee filled the air. Ava breathed in deep and stretched her limbs across the entire mattress, kicking the covers from her body. As she opened her eyes, she realized she awoke in a different place than where she'd fallen asleep.

She sat up, wondering how she'd gotten there. Did she sleepwalk there? Did Jonas and Sawyer make it home from the bar okay?

Someone did, because coffee's made.

Extending her hand to Jonas's side of the bed, she felt for warmth. Cool to the touch. She had no way of knowing whether he'd slept with her and woken early, or never came to bed at all. She reached for her cell on the nightstand and checked the time.

Blinking and adjusting the distance between the screen and her eyes, she couldn't believe she'd slept this late. She hadn't slept past ten a.m. in years. Why didn't Jonas wake her?

Ava slid off the bed and dressed in a hurry. She felt bad that Jonas had probably fed the animals without her, and wondered if Sawyer had lent a hand in her stead. He'd always been a hard worker, as long as it didn't involve housecleaning.

She glanced at herself in the mirror and cringed at her reflection. The streaks of mascara beneath her eyes bared the truth of her long emotional night. It was because of that hard cry that she'd slept as well as she had. Ready to forget her moment of weakness, she blotted a cotton ball with makeup remover and erased the evidence marring her skin.

After brushing her teeth and pulling her hair up in a ponytail, she headed into the living room. Sawyer's luggage sat on the floor, unzipped, clothes spilling out. She checked the spare room and saw the same. The bed was unmade, and last night's clothes spanned the floor beside it.

Typical.

As she rushed to grab a cup of coffee, she peeked out the window toward the barn, checking for signs of life. In the front lot, groups of black steers gathered around feeding troughs. Some milled about, looking for a better place to lick more grain. But nowhere among the concentrated herd or the fence line did she see Jonas or Sawyer.

Assuming they were in the barn feeding the horses, she sipped her coffee as quickly as she could and slipped on her boots. She rushed out the door and headed straight for the barn. In the back of her mind, she worried about Sawyer and how he'd react to seeing her again. She hated that he'd walked in on her but hoped he was mature enough to realize that even mothers had needs.

When she reached the barn and walked inside, she saw Jonas standing in the aisle with Winchester and Ranger. Both were brushed as slick as a whistle and saddled.

"Well, good morning, Trick."

Ava walked up to her horse and petted his muzzle, watching Jonas as he tied down his saddlebags. "Good morning. What are you doing?"

"We," he emphasized, "are going on a ride."

"We are? But we have horses to feed and stalls to muck."

"Not today," Sawyer said as he came in from the back, manning a wheelbarrow. "I'm taking care of that for you."

Seeing her son's warm smile, a smile without disdain or judgment, lifted that awful burden from her shoulders. She had no idea what had been said between him and Jonas last night, but it was as if she hadn't embarrassed herself at all. A slate wiped clean.

Seeing the suspicion on her face, Sawyer approached her and hugged her. "You don't have to fret anymore. Everything's gonna be all right. I promise. You just go and have some fun today, and I'll be here when you get back."

"But, you just got here, and I've hardly spent any time with you."

He took her hands and kissed her knuckles. "Don't worry. We'll have all week to catch up. You just go with Jonas. Enjoy your afternoon."

Sawyer's smile was uncontainable, his mood extremely chipper. When she glanced at Jonas, she could say the same for him too. "All right, you two. What's going on here? You both are acting weird."

"What's weird is you thinking any of this is out of the ordinary," Jonas stated as he finished picking the horses' hooves. "Years ago, we used to ride out all the time. It's a beautiful day, and I thought, why not take advantage of it. Are you game?"

Jonas's plan sounded wonderful, actually. She just couldn't believe he was making time for it. "Course I'm game. But what about Sawyer?"

"I'm a big boy, Mom. I don't need you to entertain me. I came out to lend a hand because of the bear, which, by the way, has been trapped."

Ava's gaze flew to Jonas's. "Really? All three of them?"

"It appears that way. Luke called early this morning and said they're hooking up the trailers. I'd say they should be close to relocating them in Yellowstone by now." He took out his cell and brought up an image. "Look at the pic Cole sent me of the mama grizzly. She's big, isn't she? Very healthy."

Ava laughed, noticing the bunny ears Cole gave Luke as they stood next to the culvert trap that housed her. As Ava admired the beauty of Wyoming's largest predator, she remembered how Jonas had promised a day on the ridge once the bears had been captured. Thoughts of how they planned to celebrate flooded her brain. "Is this why we're riding today?"

Jonas waggled his brow and grinned as he untied the horses from the hitching post. He might not have said a word, but his mischievous expression spoke volumes about the plans he had in mind. He reached out and wrapped his arms around her from behind, planting a kiss on her neck.

"Are you ready to go?"

Jonas's warm breath and short stubble tickled her. She squirmed, but not enough to escape. Instead, she leaned her cheek against his and whispered, "Did you pack a blanket?"

"I did."

Ava felt Jonas's hands splay across her stomach in a way that felt possessive and greedy. She burned beneath his touch, a sluggish flame that was ready to ignite. Encased in his arms, she felt treasured and loved, a feeling she missed greatly.

Her body tingled as he nuzzled her hair and kissed behind her ear. She turned into him, eager to feel the warmth of his mouth, the softness of his lips. When he kissed her, she tasted mint and his skin smelled of leather and soap. She couldn't wait to experience more of the things that made Jonas McKinley so irresistible.

They spent the morning riding up hills and racing across valleys. The beautiful countryside was their playground and laughter was their release. For far too long, they went about their days working the McKinley ranch without taking the time to enjoy it. To enjoy each other.

But today was different. It was a day to do whatever they pleased, wherever they wanted, with no threat of interruptions or responsibilities. Or bears. Like teens madly in love, they flirted and laughed. They held hands as they rode through windswept plains and shallow flowing creeks, completely immersed in conversation.

After a few hours of circling through the ranch, they finally came to the lone tree on the ridge. As they stopped their horses beneath it, they took a moment to look out at the panoramic view of the valley below. Hills and meadows rolled like waves in an ocean, while the Absaroka Mountains stood broad and mighty at the distant horizon. Vibrant blue sky hovered over a rich palette of russet badlands and green foliage, with the Sunshine Reservoir glistening in the center.

"I've ridden on this ridge countless times," Jonas said, "and it's never looked more beautiful than it does today. I think it's because you're here. You bring an element of splendor with you wherever you go. And I'm a lucky man to have you."

Ava looked at him, stunned by what he'd said. Ordinarily, Jonas had a way with words, but never when it came to matters of the heart.

"I mean every word, Trick. I would never lie to you."

She smiled. "I believe you."

In a flash, he swung his legs over the horse and dismounted, coming to her. He looked up, his hands resting on her hip and thigh. "Then believe me when I tell you, there is no one I'd rather be with than you."

Gripping her waist, he helped her to dismount, all the while holding her gaze. As she looked closer, she saw her reflection in his eyes, backlit by a tumultuous storm of blue swirls and indigo fissures. Her knees weakened, and she found it hard to think and twice as hard to talk. "I feel the same."

It was a miracle she was able to say those four words.

Upon hearing her reply, he smiled so big, his dimples popped. "Wait here."

Ava watched him circle his horse and dig into his saddlebag. He pulled out a blanket and spread it beneath the tree.

As he came back for her, he looked as devilish as the day she'd first met him. A wicked grin curved his lips while he unbuttoned his shirt in a deliberate, salacious manner. Once he chucked it over his shoulder, he pulled her close and nudged his nose with hers. She braced her hands on his chest, relishing the hard muscles and smooth skin beneath her palms. She waited for him to kiss her.

But he didn't.

Instead, he scooped her up in his arms. She gasped as her feet left the ground, feeling dizzy and excited at the same time. She felt his strength as he held her securely, his warmth as he pressed her close.

He dropped to his knees and lowered her to the ground, falling on top of her. Only then did he part his lips and kiss her.

Her world spun and her heart raced. She'd been dying for this for so long that she trembled with need and nerves.

Jonas drew back and touched her cheek. "I want you, Trick."

She smiled at hearing him voice his desires. "And you're all I've ever wanted in a man. Sometimes I feel like I'm dreaming. That none of this is real."

"But it is. My love for you is as real as it gets. You were made for me, Ava. I truly believe that."

She didn't mean to tear up, but it happened. His words touched her so deeply.

Jonas wiped a tear from her cheek. "I don't want you to cry. I don't want you to *ever* cry. All I care about is making you happy."

"You do make me happy, Jonas."

"But will you let me for the rest of your life?"

Ava's bottom lip quivered. "What are you saying?"

She felt him move slightly off her and dig into his pocket. With a serious look in his eye, he held up a diamond ring, one that looked old-fashioned in style. When she looked closer, she saw a large diamond set in vintage claw prongs in the center of six accent diamonds, sparkling under the sunlight.

Is this what I think it is? It can't be.

Jonas was never the type to settle down and marry. The whole town of Meeteetse knew that. She knew that. She spent seven years in a relationship with him knowing it wasn't likely to happen.

Is it likely now?

She looked at the ring and back at him. For fear of being wrong—and heartbroken if she was—she couldn't bring herself to think Jonas intended to propose. Her body shuddered, and she found it difficult to breathe.

"This was my mother's ring, and I want you to have it. It pains me that she never got to meet you, but I know she'd approve, as you're so much like her. And normally on an occasion such as this, I would've asked your father for his blessing."

Ava gasped, covering her mouth to choke back her sobs. "Oh, Jonas."

"I know it may seem old-fashioned, but I believe before any man takes a woman's hand in marriage, he must first request it. I'm truly sorry he's not here for me to ask, as it would've been an honor. But there is another man in your life. A young man who cares for you very much and wants only the best for you. It was his approval I sought after, as it means everything to me."

Ava reached up and wiped a tear at the corner of Jonas's eye. He laughed nervously, trying to keep it together. "I'm sorry. I didn't plan on being this emotional."

She couldn't speak. All she could do was wait with bated breath for him to finish.

Jonas took a deep breath and blew it out. "You'll be happy to know that Sawyer gave his permission for me to do this. So, here goes." He took another large breath and spoke very slowly. "I, Jonas Murphy McKinley, want to give you all that I have. I want to grow old with you. I want to be in Sawyer's life. I want to bring happiness to yours. Ava Evangeline Wallace...I want to marry you."

Ava flung her arms around his neck and crushed his lips in a kiss, knocking off his cowboy hat. "Yes! Yes! Yes! I will marry you!"

Never in a million years would she have thought she was going to be Mrs. Jonas McKinley, but as he took her hand and slid the ring on her finger, her wildest dreams came true. For the rest of her life, she was going to be able to live on this ranch, love on her cowboy, and, every once in a while, make a fool of herself doing it.

She couldn't be more comfortable than that.

Chapter Twenty-three

Brody wiped the grease from his hands on a rag and looked at the hose hanging from the bleeder valve. Lying on a mechanic's creeper, he was ready to bleed the rear brake lines in Mr. Corinth's 1950 Chevy 3100 pickup truck, after he'd spent the afternoon putting on new rotors, pads, and brakes.

Mr. Corinth sat above him in the driver's seat, telling the story of how he'd broken his arm falling down the stairs. Brody already knew the gist of the tale from Jonas, but that didn't stop Mr. Corinth from vomiting the details from his point of view.

Despite that the old man had droned on and on all day, Brody didn't give him a hard time. He'd been taught to always respect his elders, and the nonstop chatter didn't inhibit him from tightening bolts or loosening screws. He could get just as much work finished with or without the noise as long as he wasn't expected to pay close attention or join in on the conversation. Lucky for him, Mr. Corinth wasn't the type to know the difference. As long as Brody made a few sounds here and there, he was good to go.

"Okay, Mr. Corinth," Brody called out, interrupting him midsentence. "I'm going to need you to pump the brake a few times and then hold it down until I tell you to stop."

"Okay, son. Here we go."

Mr. Corinth paused his story to pump the brakes, and Brody relished the sweet sound of silence. As he opened the valve with a wrench, he monitored the stream of fluid, then closed it.

"Okay, do it again. Pump and hold."

The process continued until there was no more air in the lines and Mr. Corinth's brakes felt stiff beneath his foot.

"All right, I think we got it." Brody wheeled himself out from under the truck and welcomed the sunshine on his face. Though a necessary evil, he didn't much care for the mechanics side of restoration, as it was tedious, messy, and time consuming. Not to mention that the labor itself often went unnoticed. With bodywork—the sanding, the painting, the waxing and polishing—it didn't take a professional to appreciate the hard work that went into it. He compared it to breaking a horse. With a little love and a lot of patience, the end result produced something of noticeably higher value.

As he sat up and stretched his neck, Mr. Corinth went back to talking as if he'd never missed a beat. Brody tuned him out, thinking about the front brake lines he still had to bleed before the vintage automobile would be road worthy.

"Sonny? Your little gadget thing on the seat is vibrating," Mr. Corinth said.

Brody laughed at the old man's description of his cell and jumped to his feet to take the call. Anything to get the man to be quiet for a few minutes. He wiped his hands down the legs of his coveralls, but the grease hardly budged. "Could you?" Brody asked, gesturing for Mr. Corinth to answer it and put it up to his ear.

With shaky hands, the old man picked up Brody's cell and squinted at the screen. "How do I answer this thing? Do I push this one right here?" Mr. Corinth asked, pointing.

The name on the screen shocked Brody.

It was Liv's.

His heart kicked into high gear. He hadn't spoken to her in weeks and had begun to think Rod was right. Perhaps she had forgotten all about him in her pursuit of stardom. But seeing her name pop up on his phone sent him reeling.

"Yes, Mr. Corinth. That one. Swipe it."

"Huh? Swipe, you say?"

"Yes, sir. Swipe the screen."

Mr. Corinth dragged his finger across the display and tucked it between Brody's shoulder and his ear. Brody fought to keep the slim device pinched but gave the old man a thumbs-up as he walked a few steps away from the truck cab.

"Hello? Hello? Liv? You there?"

"Hey, Brody! How are you?"

Brody beamed at hearing her voice. "I'm much better now. How's Nashville?"

"Nashville is amazing! It's the most unbelievable place I've ever been to. Every day is a rush. I've been recording and singing and writing and singing some more…and then, just the other day, I had a photo shoot for the cover of the album. It's all happening so fast."

Brody was happy for her, as he knew how much this meant to her. She'd been chasing this dream ever since she realized she could belt out a tune. But a part of his heart ached because he suddenly believed he might never see her again.

"I'm glad things are going well for you."

"My agent says once we finish recording, and the label decides on a release date, we'll be looking at tour sites. Can you believe that? Sometime next year, I'm going to be on tour!"

Brody paced the yard, kicking at a stone on the ground. "That...that's amazing."

"Oh, Brody, it is," she said. "But there's just one thing that sucks."

Brody braced himself. He figured this was the call where she'd break it off. When she was going to tell him that she'd decided to move to Nashville permanently and couldn't keep up their long-distance relationship. He tried not to be so pessimistic, as they'd been close friends all their lives. But holding on to Liv felt like gripping sand. "What's that?"

"You're not here. With me," she said in that sweet, lovely voice Brody loved so much. "And I miss you. Really bad, Galven."

Brody closed his eyes and blew out a long breath. He felt relieved to know he'd been on her mind as much as she was on his. "I miss you too, Liv. When can I see you?"

"Oh, I don't know. I guess it depends on how fast you can drive."

"What?" Grease and brake fluid be damned, he grabbed the phone off his shoulder. "What do you mean how fast I can drive? Where are you?"

He heard Liv giggle on the other end. "On my mama's front porch."

THE END

AUTHOR'S NOTE

Did you know there's a Mavericks of Meeteetse novella that introduces some of the hunky cowboys who work the McKinley Ranch?

If not, then check out *Longing for Langston* and fall in love with Meeteetse's bad boy, Brody Galven (one of the hired hands) and his best friend, Liv Langston. In that story, you'll get to know how their relationship started and why they're in the midst of a long-distance relationship.

If you've already read *Longing For Langston* and have enjoyed *Made For McKinley*, then I encourage you to read the continuing books in the series to find out more about Jonas's and Ava's engagement, and the possibility of Brody's and Liv's relationship finally heating up.

*All are meant to be stand-alones (and can be read in any order), but for a more satisfying "happily ever after," reading in order is helpful and encouraged.

****

Take a trip out West and meet Brody, Jonas, Cole, and Sawyer—the four sexy, rugged cowboys who rope and run the McKinley ranch, as well as the women who try to tame them.

MAVERICKS OF MEETEETSE

A cowboy romance series set in the small town of
Meeteetse, Wyoming.

Longing for Langston, Novella Book 1
Made for McKinley, Book 2
Falling for Forester, Book 3
Wild for Wallace, Book 4

LONGING FOR LANGSTON
Mavericks of Meeteetse, Novella Book 1 (Brody & Liv)

Tired of living in his brother's shadow, Brody Galven wants the folks of Meeteetse to realize he's no longer a bad boy screwup. He also wants his childhood best friend, Olivia Langston. While staying out of trouble proves impossible, admitting he loves her is out of the question...even when she's about to walk out of his life forever.

FALLING FOR FORESTER
Mavericks of Meeteetse, Book 3 (Cole & Crys)

Cowboy cattle rancher Cole Forester likes things the way they are—quiet, no-frills, and uncomplicated. He's a glorified bachelor with only a dog as his companion, totally content to live a solitary life next to the McKinley ranch. That is until a cute little barrel racer shows up looking for a job as a ranch hand.

Tomboy Crys Willingham hangs up her rodeo hat and heads to where her friend Ava Wallace lives, hoping to score a job that doesn't involve the risk of broken bones every time she mounts up. Once she lays eyes on Cole, it's her vulnerable heart that's in danger of breaking.

WILD FOR WALLACE
Mavericks of Meeteetse, Book 4 (Sawyer & Charlotte)

College graduate Sawyer Wallace has just come home to Meeteetse to visit with family. Excited to put his new degree to good use, he lands a comfortable job at the McKinley ranch until he can find something better. After a fluke horse accident on his watch, he calls Doc "Charlie" Peterson to the farm, only to find the highly-praised vet is a woman. Even better, she's an eligible, spicy little brunette with a jacked-up truck.

Charlotte Peterson is the only veterinarian in Meeteetse, taking over her father's practice after he retired. Traveling from ranch to ranch doesn't leave her much free time. So when the new manager of the McKinley ranch calls her to care for an injured horse, she has trouble trying to convince the handsome "greenhorn" that she has little patience for his charming antics, much less time to date. While she's determined to dodge Sawyer's every advance, she finds that some things can grow wild without cultivation.

ABOUT THE AUTHOR

RENEE VINCENT is a *USA Today* bestselling author of historical romance, contemporary romance, and women's fiction with a smidgen of spunk. From her memorable Viking warriors to her charming Alpha male heroes of modern day, readers will be whisked away to a world filled with tender moments, gripping adventure, unpredictable plot twists, and undying love. Her books have earned numerous accolades, including a #1 Bestseller for Viking Romance.

She lives on a secluded hundred-acre horse farm in the rolling hills of Kentucky with her husband, two beautiful daughters, and a cat who thinks he's the master of the house.

www.ReneeVincent.com

Books By Series

Vikings of Honor Series
Sunset Fire, Book 1
Emerald Glory, Book 2
Souls Reborn, Book 3
Tempered Steel, Book 4

Mavericks of Meeteetse Series
Longing for Langston, Brody & Liv, Book 1
Made for McKinley, Jonas & Ava, Book 2
Falling For Forester, Cole & Crys, Book 3
Wild for Wallace, Sawyer & Charlotte, Book 4

Jamett & Joseph Series
The Start of Something Good, Book 1
The Road to Something Better, Book 2
The Gift of Something Grand, Book 3

Stand Alone Novel
Silent Partner (The Sweet Version)

If you enjoyed this book by Renee Vincent, please consider leaving an honest review at your favorite vendor. Reviews not only give credibility to an author's work, they also help other readers find quality books worth reading.

ReneeVincent.com

Made in the USA
Lexington, KY
28 April 2019